THE PHOENIX ARCHER

ARCHER

By Matt Latimer

THE IRISH FIELD ARCHERY

Publishing

I would like to begin by thanking all the readers of The Irish Field Archery Monthly who brought to life a great magazine which I have the pleasure to write for.

And extend my thanks to Marcin Malek for letting me do this serial, not forgetting Katherine Robinson for taking the time to proof all of this, doing so with so much else going on, and for the constant encouragement. My first fan, and a great trad archer.

For Billy 'Shim' Latimer,
who made this small part of the world safer for us.

And for archers, the world over.

Matt Latimer

The Phoenix archer

©

Copy right by Matt Latimer

First edition

Published by TIFAM CLG Publishing

Portlaoise 2024, Ireland

(with Staten House)

ISBN: 979-8-89587-906-1

Proofreading by Katherine Robinson

Front Cover art by Glenn Thompson

Technical editor: Marcin Małek

Table of Contents

Editor's preface

Dear Readers, Friends, Archers,

There are books that don't merely rest on the stiff confines of your bookshelf, waiting to be forgotten amidst the clutter of ordinary life. No, some books wedge themselves between your ribs, rooting in the tender hollows of your chest, their pulse entwining with your own, as if challenging you to ever let them go. Matt Latimer's The Phoenix Archer is precisely such a book. It doesn't deign to be merely read. It insists upon being devoured, absorbed—not unlike breath itself, not unlike blood. And resist, you won't. Once its ink-stained tendrils seize you, escape becomes less a possibility and more a daydream you wouldn't bother entertaining.

And what of this world Latimer crafts—this Anordaithe, a realm so wildly alive it thrums with its own feral heartbeat? It is no mere invention. It is a resurrection, a reclamation, a hymn to the ancient battles between humankind's greed and nature's quiet dignity. Latimer does not sketch its contours with the detached precision of a cartographer, no cold grids or measured lines here. Instead, he summons it forth with the ardour of a bard, a voice rising above the mist. The forests do not simply sway; they heave and shudder as if burdened by the weight of untold sagas. The rivers? They are restless veins, pulsating with secrets too immense for their banks to hold. To enter Anordaithe is not merely to read about it but to stumble into it, to feel its spectral breath curl against the nape of your neck, its shadows unfurl across your thoughts like creeping ivy.

Within this wild expanse, three lives emerge, tethered to one another by threads both fragile and unbreakable. Alejandro Zaragosa, Ksenia Kiamount, Blair Ruthvane—names that will soon etch themselves into the marrow of your memory. Alejandro, the titular Phoenix Archer, does not wield his bow as a mere weapon but as an extension of his very soul. Each arrow, a cry, a prayer, a blazing contradiction of vengeance and sorrow. And Ksenia —ah, she is the wind incarnate, untamed and unpredictable, as likely to raze as she is to heal. Her loyalties are fleeting as frost on an autumn morning, and yet they burn with an intensity that defies their brevity. And Blair? Blair's strength is quieter, softer— a stubborn resilience that endures when all else falters. Together, they are a constellation of flawed brilliance, jagged pieces struggling to align within a universe that does not care for perfection.

But to speak of The Phoenix Archer solely in terms of its characters is to do it a grave disservice. For this is a story not just of individuals but of themes ancient and raw, vibrating across the human condition like the string of a bow drawn taut. The act of archery, silent yet electric, becomes a metaphor for our eternal grappling with chaos and control, intention and consequence. In Latimer's hands, the bowstring becomes not just a tool but a philosophy. To draw it is to face uncertainty with courage. To release it is to leap into the abyss of faith, trusting in nothing but the fleeting arc of the arrow. Within that brief trajectory lies all of life—its wild unpredictability, its relentless momentum, its bittersweet finality.

Latimer's prose is an act of alchemy, words transfigured into a visceral, near-cinematic _experience. He writes with the precision of a fletcher shaping an arrow, every sentence honed, every image sharpened to a fine point. Yet there is nothing sterile here. His words are alive, restless, feral. Dialogue brims with the tang of truth, an authenticity that crackles like kindling caught alight. The grandeur of Anordaithe is rendered in strokes both broad and intimate—landscapes painted in the boldest hues yet whispered through the finest of details. Every line carries the weight of its world, yet none of it feels heavy. Instead, you are swept along, a willing captive of its current._

What sets this book apart, what elevates it to something rare and precious, is its refusal to patronize with simplicity. Latimer does not peddle heroes draped in untarnished glory or villains skulking in caricatured malice. His characters are real, achingly so—blemished and broken, noble and selfish, contradictions that feel like home. Right and wrong weave together in a tapestry so intricate that you cannot pull at a single thread without unravelling the whole. This is not a tale of resolution; it is one of reckoning. It mirrors humanity in all its *messy, defiant beauty—a thing fractured, yet somehow whole.*

As a writer—and an archer—this story resonates with me in ways that feel uncomfortably intimate. The rhythm of Latimer's narrative mirrors the rhythm of the bowstring: the taut alignment of mind and muscle, the electric stillness before release, the ecstasy and ache of letting go. To read The Phoenix Archer is to participate, not passively observe. It demands your engagement, your introspection, even as it withholds easy answers. And isn't that what the finest stories should do?

Latimer, as I've come to know him, is a craftsman of rare humility, a mind that treads fearlessly into shadow and returns bearing truths both luminous and unsettling. His gift lies not in cleverness but in a relentless honesty that seeps into every line of this tale. The Phoenix Archer is a testament to storytelling's power not just to entertain but to connect—to provoke, to endure, to matter.

So to you, readers of Matt's book, I say this: you will not merely read this book. You will live it, breathe it, ache for it. Whether you are an archer who understands the sacred ritual of a bowstring drawn or a dreamer seeking the thrill of discovery, The Phoenix Archer will speak to you in ways you won't soon forget.

Latimer has gifted us a story, and I, in turn, am honoured to gift it to you. Step into Anordaithe, let its wild beauty claim you, and perhaps, as the final page turns, you will find yourself forever altered.

Yours in wonder,
Marcin Małek
TIFAM Editor-in-Chief

Prologue – The Ivory Griffin

The world – Anordaithe; land, water, light, darkness, atmosphere, and throughout it all, life. Sculpted by beings of incomprehensible power, or by nature itself, most people have an opinion. For some, it hardly matters. The mystery only adds to the beauty of Anordaithe and life itself.

Five continents dominate Anordaithe: The Crown, The Sigal, The Scar, The Maw, and the largest of them all, The Mane.

The last of these is unlike the others. The Mane stands as a vast world onto itself, encompassing no fewer than fifty nations, kingdoms, republics, and tribal worlds, across forests, rain forests, mountains, jungles, deserts, and lakes as large as any country. But, more famously, is the presence of a singular archer. One who is embedded in legend, and contempt, the Phoenix Archer.

Garvey Sathid, a prince from the Dytrentian Empire, in some far off, obscure manner, was secretly an insecure man. To anyone on the outside, being born into the mighty Dytrentian Empire that dominated The Maw, would seem to automatically place a person on a pedestal – especially considering the way they would walk over those around them.

He was middle-aged, reaching the point in life when maintaining one's level of fitness gradually becomes a losing battle. Despite this, the prince threw himself into many challenging ventures. A hardy Dytrentian upbringing kept the muscles strong and the heart pumping, while encouraging cunning and guile. Manipulation and exploitation of guards, mercenaries, and friends in high places had been his primary method of social climbing to greater standing, and in keeping his hold on it – however little.

To compensate for his lower standing, Garvey travelled far, hunting the largest and most dangerous creatures he could find. Proudly, he boasted of his alleged prowess through his taxidermies, or trophies.

However, despite his efforts in the grotesque field of game hunting, Garvey's path had met a crippling social barrier: no-one really cared. Despite the titans and predators, he brought home, Garvey did not belong to the right circles for anyone to give him the time of day. Frustrated, he then threw himself into the challenge of earning a place within the most prestigious hunting organisation Anordaithe-over: the Flint Castle.

Tragically, the Castle claimed their actions were that of conservation, declaring that no-one could respect nature more than they. Yet, a pair of ashen mountain bears from Besdenu – a species renowned for their uniquely patterned fur – flanked the entrance to their main lodge. To most, this spoke volumes regarding their intentions, as the species was listed as functionally extinct.

There were only a few hundred members of the Flint Castle. At the Head of the Organisation were twelve elite members, four of which were descendants of founding members. Together, they sat in judgment of aspiring hunters. Regardless of the rare and mighty animals Garvey brought to the Castle, none seemed to satisfy the Twelve's lunacy.

Garvey ordered scouts from his private army to search for potential game. Venturing outwards, to the mountain ranges of Bravenasil, a nation in the southeast of The Mane, they reported uncountable numbers of griffins residing there. Many were species they had never seen before, including one extraordinary griffin, they named the Ivory Griffin.

Its feathers and fur were ivory white, its eyes gleamed like rubies, the avian talons like molten gold, and the feline claws, jet. They stated it could easily have been mistaken for a celestial being, and speculated if any foreign god or demigod owned it.

After getting word of this animal, Garvey had an epiphany. It was something utterly unique and once in, not just a generation, but many generations. This was going to win him his place within the Flint Castle.

Now, at the trampled path, leading upwards to the darkening silver mountains, Garvey's hunting party had become wary. Griffins, part bird of prey, part big cat, encompassed the most lethal traits of two of Anordaithe's most ferocious animals. The species were in the thousands and whilst some were harmless, most would snatch a tender human from the ground. The smallest recorded griffin was three metres long, and the largest twenty. But their size and gait were contrary to their grace and deftness.

Garvey had never hunted one before, and thought, how hard could it be to take one from the skies? They're huge, and there is nothing up there for them to hide behind.

He looked forward to an effortless entry to the Castle, with his crossbow; a device built from rare metals stolen by his Empire's greed. It was enchanted to launch the bolt with the sheer force of being hit by a landslide. The exterior of the beast would remain pristine, whilst the organs took the trauma. Greater evidence of the Empire's sacrilegious ways, its wooden frame had been sculpted from a shrine that had been built by pagan naturalists, who worshiped nature as their deity. Not that it mattered to Garvey, as that culture had been purged.

Looking back at his entourage, Garvey was far from satisfied with their efforts. He suspected that they were deliberately impeding his progress, out of a misguided fear of the animals. Several of the men with him were Dytrentian soldiers, but the rest were slaves.

The slaves pulled a ballista, some five meters long that could shoot a dragon from the sky. But this was not to be used on his trophy, as he wanted the whole body intact to adorn his throne room – the one he envisioned in his mind – and for the Castle and Empire to see.

In the event one of the much larger species attacked, the ballista was to be called in, but until then, the high-powered crossbows he and his soldiers wielded would suffice. The slaves were not armed, as weapons in the Dytrentian Empire could only be used by those who had been deemed citizens – and Garvey and his bodyguards were outnumbered by them, not to mention, far from the safety of the Empire.

Hours went by. The group laboured upwards, past magnificent views of silver valleys speckled with skeletal ruins, snow enriching everything it touched. However, this was lost to Garvey, who was furious that not a single griffin had so much has been heard. This was, naturally, the fault of everyone but himself; the slaves too slow and frightened, the soldiers making too much noise or not paying enough attention.

They took a break by a frozen lake, the pale blue sheet a canvas for the jagged, thorny peeks surrounding them. Garvey began to curse at how barren these lands seemed to be; what bounty was there? They had ascended to a much higher altitude, but not a griffin was present.

These thoughts were lost in an instant as the ballista, thirty metres to his right, exploded in a violent plume of fire and jet-black smoke. From its base, jagged spears of amber ripped outwards in many directions, leaving paths consumed by an abyssal blackness.

The slaves fled as if a predator was at their heels, despite the soldiers' threats. Their barking didn't last long - once the erratic path of the amber claws met the first soldier, he combusted into a bonfire, shrieking as armour became molten, and fused with flesh. A second went up in the same abrupt manner, his body exploding outwards in raging, ravenous flames. He charged straight off the path they had come up, into a ravine.

Only one soldier remained next to Garvey. "We... we need to go, your highness..." The final soldier pleaded, before an arrow struck his throat with a wet sounding *thump*. He staggered a few steps, one hand wrapped around the protruding shaft, eyes bright with alarm, and fell back. His own wide and frightened eyes still on the dead soldier, Garvey tried to flee, but turned, sprinting straight into a fist and was unconscious before knowing what happened.

As he came to, fragments of what had happened, like shards of glass, pierced through the fog in Garvey's mind. Instinctively, he tried to lash out, but found his hands bound behind his back. As his struggle tilted him onto one side, a mountainous weight of cold fell over him, stiffening his whole body. From the dazzling and painful white light forming the entrance to a cave, came a silhouette.

"Who are you!?" Garvey cried, unable to hide the panic in his voice. "I am a prince of Dytrentia!" He continued desperately as if it meant something. Despite his binds, the cold had him restrained, with its deep and aching numbness surrounding his limbs, torso, and face.

A sigh came from the shadowed figure before he stepped forward into plainer view. As he did so, he set a bow against the cave wall, removed his back quiver, and lazily, hanged it on an outward jutting rock. This archer was a man of average height, wearing a tunic laced with white fur, black breeches diffusing into green towards heavy boots. A rich orange scarf had been pulled up over the lower part of his face.

With a hard voice, he spoke, "Are you speaking ironically?" The tone was staggered, each word very enunciated with effort. "The only

15

The Phoenix Archer   Matt Latimer

power and strength in these mountains are their griffin inhabitants."

This stranger crouched in front of Garvey, his cool grey eyes boring into him, with the careful study of a predator. There was silence, and the man pulled down his scarf, revealing the left of his face to be a glassy smear of burn scars. These stretched from the edge of his mouth over his cheek and went down his neck. On the other side of his face, faint black stubble grew and stretched to meet the barren boarders of the scar tissue.

"What do you want?" Garvey pleaded, his eyes seeing only the wicked, searing scars.

"I believe you may have been told about me," he replied, standing back up, the hard-pressed words clearly related to the injuries about his face and jaw.

"I am *prince* Garvey, to you!" Garvey seethed reflectively, but the venom was lost on the archer, who just looked at him thoughtfully.

"Other than being born into royalty, what did you do actually do to earn that title?" Only the right side of the archer's mouth moved as he spoke, the left paralysed.

There was silence, in part because the ravaging cold was eating away at the little energy Garvey had left.

"I thought so. Entitlement is ugly," the archer went on.

"*You're* the phoenix they all talked about!" Garvey managed to blurt out, regretting the burst of energy as the dry cold invaded his mouth and throat.

"You're not the first Dytrentian I've met, you know. Twenty years ago, in a place called Eitimovel, legions of you tried to take a town because you wanted the people there as slaves. I happened to be passing through when your invasion began," the archer explained, leaning down, casting a shadow as cold as the grave. The slower speech was grating on the hunter, each second like an icy razor scratching over his skin.

"I wasn't prepared to let you take those people. I stood on a hill overlooking a vast legion and took the only weapon I had; a bow, built by gods, or so I'm told, who have long since left this world, and arrows, fletched with the feathers of a phoenix." The archer gestured to the far wall upon which the bow rested. Sitting on a leather wrap, were a dozen arrows, their flights burning like the horizon breaking through a night's storm.

The archer sighed. "Regrettably, I didn't have the protective garments I wear today," he tugged at the leather scarf before holding up his left hand, which was as severely scarred as his face. "I found out the hard way that leather, from a sea-leviathan, was also required if anyone was to loose these arrows."

"Gods? Primitive ape..." Garvey frothed, now panting uncontrollably, every breath burning through the back of his throat.

The archer ignored him and continued. "The legions came forward, and like you witnessed today, they burned and screamed. I'm sure it was like a symphony to Eitimovel's Gods of Death and War. I couldn't hold them forever, as I only had a dozen of the arrows and after the first was in sheer anguish. Mercy, I thought I was dying. But I killed enough of your soldiers, and the people in the town escaped."

By now, Garvey's extremities had lost all feeling, his fingers ghostly white with an abrasive blue rimming his nails and bruising the joints of his fingers. Garvey had heard only fables of archers using phoenix fletched arrows, elaborate lies. The animals were immortal, indestructible. The closest they came to death was during a moulting phase, in which they entered a comatose-like state, before awakening with a new array of fiery feathers. They incinerated anything they came close to. In Anordaithe, they had their own lands, and only the insane went looking to find one.

"You think above all others, that you have ownership to Anordaithe, don't you? That it all falls under your domain, and by extension everything which resides there."

"Who are you, really!? I am Dytrentian; I am part of a people who have striven to rise above all others, be they man or beast!" Garvey dropped his head, finally breaking eye contact with the archer who took a few steps away from him.

"Why are you the one tied up then? Your bodyguards are dead, and the men you called slaves, have fled."

"You are interfering with nature! It is our right, by sheer force of will above all others, or by Gods, whatever you believe in, that we have dominion over all creatures! There is nothing more natural than asserting our dominance and control – it's the way we're made. If we don't, then we are interfering with that natural order! We control dangerous animal populations, and we keep them from harming people!"

The archer spoke, turning his back to Garvey. "Conservation? Population control? Whatever excuses you make, they're a façade. All you want is to build your own image up and up and up, until people have no choice but to see it... And if you want to talk about harming the innocent, what carnage has your empire wrought?"

"How much human blood did you spill today!? Don't you dare try to claim not to be a hypocrite here!"

The archer smirked without mirth. "I don't deny taking life, goodness; I've taken plenty of Dytrentian lives... But the Castle seeks to ravage nature for their own ego and lust. So, like a bear, naturally designed to keep deer populations in check, *we* keep *you* in check."

"Who's we?" Garvey pondered to himself for a moment before continuing. "We have every right to hold dominion-"

"So, you said," the archer retorted with a weary sigh. "Don't go repeating yourself. How many species have been hunted into extinction? How many *people* have died or been displaced because their food sources were hunted to extinction? Tell me where the conservation is!" He continued, marching back towards Garvey with a tread as heavy as any cave bear.

"What about the wealth?" Garvey answered. "The Castle pays with wealth that even a prince like me is in awe of... I have given more money than you could ever know, to hunt in places that needed it. Do you know how much I donated to this government, here? Or what the price of a griffin is, even a minor one?" Garvey began to chuckle to himself as fear and fatigue increased its hold.

"And where does all this money go? Schools? Farmers?"

There was an uneasy silence as Garvey tried to form an answer. No sound materialised, despite his moving lips.

"Of course not, it lines the pockets of politicians, rulers, leaders, whoever. The poor remain poor, the starving, starving, and the sick, sick."

"Please! Look, just let me go and I'll - I'll leave your mountains then... And I'll make sure the wealth goes where it's supposed to. I'm Dytrentian, and we wouldn't want to see our wealth misused."

"These are not *my* mountains," the archer stated. "Haven't you been listening? They belong to nature. And what about the other lands and animals? You think you have the right to lust over the deaths of creatures that often can't defend themselves?"

"Have you seen what a chronosaurs can do!? What a sea leviathan does? Whole merchant fleets obliterated. Livelihoods gone. Families extinguished," Garvey added wildly.

"And you accused me of hypocrisy. You just described your Empire. Stop pretending that your lust and ego aren't the real reasons here. In a world where a chronosaurs no longer harmed anyone, or where we didn't expand into their lands, would you and the Castle stop killing them? Remember, this is a *sport* for you. And how many animals have you slaughtered that *are* harmless to you? I hunt, of course. We are, after all, omnivores, but killing an old deer out of necessity compared to killing a lion for the enjoyment of it are *very* different; a lack of respect for life, nature, and wasteful – utterly so – and perverse."

"So, what?" Garvey spat, losing all composure, as the stress of his capture finally overwhelmed him in agonising waves. "So, what, if I enjoy it? I need it. We have might and the strength, and you know what else? The right! Nature, as you fetishize her, gave us that! We rose above all others, even whatever sub-species of human you are! Can you explain that?"

"No, Garvey, nature did not, as you are about to see."

Now, Garvey's guts turned as cripplingly cold as the rest of him. He began to protest, but the archer took a harsh hold of his throat, cutting off the ability to do anything other than gurgle. Garvey was dragged forwards. A flint knife was pulled from a sheath on the archer's waist and the bonds around Garvey's wrists cut.

With a sharp tug to the scalp, Garvey found himself being thrown forwards towards the glowing entrance of the cave. Silver and ivory shades assaulted his vision in vivid blurs.

"Where are we going?" He whimpered pitifully, as he felt the barbed lashes of the winter outside, its talons of ice reaching for him.

"Do you know why in all the hours you spent ascending the mountain, you never saw griffins?"

"I..." Now the cold was beginning to rob him of the ability to form coherent sentences.

"I was following you. The heat of the phoenix feathers tends to keep many other animals away, you see; they sense it and know the heat belongs to something much bigger and more dangerous – which is fascinating, when you consider that no griffin here will have ever seen a phoenix."

The archer shoved Garvey into the open, and he staggered forwards. Daylight continued to flare before his eyes, before settling to reveal a plateau half a mile wide and just as long. Yet the scenery was lost on Garvey. Before him, perched with resounding majesty and sitting upright like a cat, was the Ivory Griffin.

The golden beak opened, wide enough for someone to stand in, and a shriek of ear-splitting menace came forth as it sensed the heat of the arrows in the archer's back quiver. The animal shied away, backwards, keeping its intense red eyes locked onto both men. Its back arched sharply, its head and golden maw lowered.

Unsurprisingly, Garvey soiled himself at the sight and sound of the griffin. He fell to his knees. He turned back to the archer and began pleading for him not to leave, trembling hands reaching out and falling shy of the archer.

"Here, Garvey, mighty prince of Dytrentia, aspiring for greater things, is your prize," he said wearily throwing a hand towards the animal. "Go and prove that you _stand_ above nature, that you've conquered her, too."

"No, please, no... Look, I'll give you anything! What's the price of this animal?"

The look in return was a blend of pity and frustration.

"What have I been saying? These animals, they do _not_ have a price," the archer seethed, clutching Garvey's jaw with a gloved hand. Slowly his head was brought around to see the wide spread of griffins, all watching them and waiting patiently for something to happen. Some softly kneaded their talons into the dirt, others yawned with apparent boredom or groomed themselves, long bright tongues going over chest fur and feathers.

Garvey's eyes couldn't see anything other than the yellow beaks and black talons, and the amber brown eyes already devouring him.

The archer shoved Garvey away and marched past him, "This is, Garvey, your shot at the Castle, at whatever it is you wish to achieve in life..."

"No, gods, no, don't leave me!" He cried, trying to run. He slipped in his own mess instead and fell to the ground. And, having spent the last of his energy, Garvey lost the ability to do anything other than whimper.

The archer walked nonchalantly past the Ivory Griffin and paused for a moment next to it. With only one half of his face still alive with nerves, he smiled a half-smile and then walked on.

Orion Aldenberg, the Chief of the Flint Castle was in his vast office, as he always was in the late afternoon. No work was being done, but he always took the time to enjoy the peaceful serenity. The rich gold of the setting sunlight poured over him from the wide and tall viewing window making up the rear wall.

The string of a bow slipped from his fingers as he drew his elbow back. The arrow sliced gracefully through the air, before thudding into the large mock-target of a hydra, which broke up the waves of light pouring into the office. A perfect hit, puncturing the neck joint just under the jaw of the far-right head.

This routine ensured Luciana Doran, the secretary of the Flint Castle, knew where to find him. She was a tall and broad-shouldered woman with pale skin, a flat, but narrow nose and eyes the colour of wet grass. Muddy coloured hair fell past her shoulders, streaked with bright red dye.

"Ori, it's been far too long a day, and I want to get this final item done, so I can disappear into a tavern somewhere. Prince Sathid was reported missing," she began, entering though the arching doors; eight-foot-tall brass barriers inlaid with scenes of famous hunts throughout the Castle's long history, further embellished by precious metals.

Orion looked around from the analysis of his shot, only his head turning. With the broken arcs of golden light pouring over him, and the silhouetted mock-up of the serpent creature framing the scene, the Chief looked a man out of myth. Not his intention, as Orion preferred to stay grounded, saving the dangers of hubris for amateurs. He glanced at her with mild curiosity. A man of tact and directness, he waited to hear more before deciding to say anything, Luci knew.

The Chief of the Flint Castle was tall and lean, moving with the kind of grace and strength seen in a large feline, circling another predator. In recent years, since winning the vote to lead the Castle, his dark blonde beard had been neatly trimmed, much to his chagrin. Orion preferred the unkempt look to match the untamed wilds. He kept his head shaved for practical reasons, to keep hair out of his eyes, and to prevent lice or any other disgusting creatures from impairing a hunt. His right eye – a worn bronze to match his remaining natural eye – was artificial, an enchanted prosthetic granting sight. But the skin around the socket was perpetually bruised with a light purple tint.

"This was a few days ago, but now, friends of ours have found evidence suggesting most people in line to become the new Dytrentian Emperor are now a step closer to realising their megalomaniacal dreams."

She stopped by the desk and fell into a crocodile-leather upholstered chair opposite the Chief with a deep sigh, spilling both arms over the sides.

"Our members and aspirants go missing every now and again, especially in The Mane," Orion replied cooly, looking hardly interested in the information, but lowering his longbow and turning fully to face Luci out of good manners. Obviously, he would not allow himself to get his hopes up just yet.

"At least, what, a third of it is still uncharted?" He unslung the quiver from his waist, the rich silvery feathers of the flights glinting, their razor barbs capable of slicing cleaning through surfaces as tough as leather. The quiver was set neatly on his red-wood desk, to the side.

The target of the hydra towered over him, with its three heads held high, almost reaching the ceiling, seven metres from the dark grey wooden floor. Their fangs were sculpted and painted to give the realistic impression of dripping, acidic venom. Snarls conveyed a hate, derived from the knowledge that their home had been intruded upon – or so Luci thought. Every vivid violet scale that made up the ridges of the head crests and neck contrasted against the subdued bronze colours of the rest of the body. Scales glinted like warning beacons, and the blackness of the eyes, were like whirlpools drowning any surrounding light or hope. Ivory horns broke through the near-impenetrable skin, ordaining the crowns of the heads, running down the serpentine necks and over their shared back.

It was a frighteningly accurate copy of the beast Ori had brought in, long ago, as his means of joining the Castle. The real one, seen to, by the best taxidermists in all of Anordaithe, was in the Trophy Vault deep under their lodge, with all the other trophies brought in by aspirants.

"Well, the scouts followed the same planned path as the prince." Luci leaned forward, tilting her head. "And their mules went berserk, thew several riders off - killed two by launching them down a ravine and crippled several others."

"That's a major riling up," Orion mused quietly. His expression changed, his smouldering eyes narrowing into a darkening storm as he leaned forward and placed both arms on his desk.

"A few proceeded onwards and found what looked like a volcanic eruption," Luci went on, leaning forward even more, eyes ablaze. "Rock was smeared into glass by something, with a pitch covered crater left behind, and still simmering. The falling snow was melting to water and turning to steam before it had a chance to hit the ground."

"Could have been a dragon of some sort," Orion countered, leaning back, and folding his arms.

"Not in the mountains of Bravenasil, not even close by... And what fire-breathers are potent enough to leave heat lingering for so long?" Luci shot back.

"Well, perhaps this *finally* is something..." Orion murmured, glancing to his left, at the weapons case built into the cold stone wall of the chamber, between the immaculately polished quad-tusked mammoth skull, and the taxidermy of a five-metre wide chronosaurus foot. "The bait I laid worked..."

A frown ran over Luci's brow, turning quickly to a darkening scowl. This was news to her, and since when did Ori hold anything back? – From her? Luci had risen up through the ranks of the Flint Castle with him, and since meeting, the pair had never engaged in a hunt without the other.

"I made a deal with the Sathid Estate in Dytrentia," Orion explained, looking back from the iron-framed case to see her glaring at him. "After the prince put in his desire for membership, I was contacted by his family's representatives. Apparently, they were getting fed up with his silly little adventures, especially with his brothers and sisters off campaigning too. They were worried he would try to upstage their military achievements. So, they sent the Castle a king's ransom to see he disappeared."

"Are you kidding?" Luci replied, disgust and contempt rolling from her in tangible waves. It was an ugly, underhanded move, and, beneath Orion, frankly. But still, one fewer Dytrentian in Anordaithe was never a bad thing. "We're assassins now? This had better be a one off, Ori!" She snapped, as if berating a sibling.

Orion held his hands up placatingly as Luci simmered in her seat. "I let it leak to his guides about the fabled Ivory Griffin in the hope to get prince Sathid over there. This won't happen again, Luci. A one off. But like I said, our members and aspirants have been going missing in The Mane for as long as the Castle has hunted there."

"You laid down bait to see if *he* would step out into the open for a sighting." Luci paused for a moment, processing this new information. "Well, it seems to have worked."

"Better a Dytrentian, and an aspirant at that, than one of our members, right?"

"How much is a Dytrentian prince worth?"

"Exclusive hunting rights across their empire, and a galleon of gold in donations to our organisation... We even got to keep the ship. But you know what this *means*, Luci. All the gold and game in Anordaithe, I'd give it all up if I had it, for this."

Again, he looked to the weapons case, to the item contained within, an item of legend which only she and he knew existed.

"What about current members over there? Do we warn them, or call them back?"

"Strictly speaking, we don't have the authority to tell our members no on sanctioned hunts. We manage the Castle; this isn't a military organisation. Warn them, yes, hide them away when they overstep into a region which we're not welcome in, of course. But leave everything as it is."

Luci nodded gently, dropping her gaze for a moment. She glanced back up to meet Orion's clear eyes. "Okay. When are we leaving?"

Part I – The Mirrored Draig

Ksenia Kiamount stepped into the tavern. Her dark-orange eyes glinted as she scanned the room, landing on a hunched figure, sitting alone in a gloomy corner.

"You owe me a drink," she spoke. The man looked up from the tome he was reading, half of his face in shadow.

"How do I owe *you* a drink?" He replied, each word strained. "But I could use another away." He shrugged, holding up two fingers towards the bar. The tavern owner came over and poured two tankards. Ksenia sat, resting her chin on her hand.

"The Dytrentian Empire is a bit riled up," she said casually.

"Oh?" the man replied, indifferently.

The darkness slipped from him, revealing glassy scars, spread over the left side of his face and neck. His short black beard came to a blunt stop as it met the scars. Those easily offended would recoil at the sight, but not Ksenia.

"Yeah, I let slip that a prince was looking to poach a griffin. He's gone missing." She had no idea how the information had reached Alejandro, known better as the Phoenix Archer.

"Sounds like you're responsible; throwing around privileged information," Alejandro teased, a half grin appearing, as one side of his face remained frozen.

"Dytrentian nobility is furious," Ksenia continued. "At least, putting on a show about being furious. It'll be old news by the time we finish these ales." *Typical of the Dytrentians*, she thought. *Bury anything that could be considered weakness.* "They've put him down as *missing*, but everyone has their minds made up."

She sighed.

"It's so good to see you again," Ksenia murmured, trying to recall when she'd last seen Alejandro. There was a weary demeanour about him as he leaned against the cool stone wall. Yet, his speed and ferocity were as unrelenting as his namesake beast.

The pair were the same age, in their early forties, though Ksenia lacked the hard-worn features of Alejandro.

"And you, Ksenia. How is your colourful sanctuary?" His slow manner of speaking required his audience to be patient.

The Kiamount Sanctuary was Ksenia's livelihood, and her family's legacy. It sought to ensure the protection of all avians, and anything else that can fly. Specialist breeding programmes and animal tracking were Ksenia's talents as she kept species safe from poaching and trafficking too.

"Very well, but that's not what I want to talk to you about." Ksenia tilted her tankard towards Alejandro. He leaned forward, the creaking of his chair breaking the silence.

She dropped her voice instinctively. "There's a new species of dusk draig – towards the Ceiho border," Ksenia began. "Border guards have been sending messengers to the Capital with sightings."

"Ordinarily; wonderful. But you aren't typically a bearer of good news," Alejandro replied, sombrely. The comment squeezed at Ksenia's chest, though, he was correct.

"That's not true. Don't forget, I'm your source of rare wine," she replied with a wry grin. "Unfortunately, a Castle member has taken it upon herself to be the first to claim one."

"Where are you getting this information from?"

"An associate at the museum and a friend in military administration. The border guards are open to bribes from the Castle."

"Turning a blind eye to illegal hunts."

Smaller dragons residing within Bravenasil were hunted for sport, often receiving excruciating deaths.

"This species, it's said to be ten metres long, fire breathing, which is actually rare out there, given the heat. Its scales and feathers shine like a mirror..." Ksenia's voice trailed off as she became lost in the beauty being woven together in her mind.

"It's almost invisible then... No wonder it's only recently been discovered. Bigger and brighter animals have gone undiscovered for centuries," Alejandro spoke quietly.

"You'd be surprised how indifferent most draigs are to people. They like to be left to themselves." A thoughtful look passed over the right side of Alejandro's face. "Anyway, the sightings were by the ruins of Old Gadav, you know them?"

"Of course, I do."

"Don't forget your *good* arrows. Their heat may be our saving grace where fangs and talons are concerned." The heat from the phoenix feathers would ward off most animals, due to instinctual fear.

"All my arrows are good." Alejandro grinned.

The northwest border with Ceiho was flat and arid. Despite its barren appearance, the land was rich with life. Sparse pockets of vegetation were scattered throughout, casting shadows across the land. Within these shadows, big cats, boar, deer, and huge flightless birds could be found avoiding the heat.

"Artless..." Alejandro sighed.

The pair were prone on a mound, an island in a long, dried-up lake. Rusty red rocks rose about them, arching overhead. Already, the pair were caked in dust, their mouths dry. Two hundred yards away, within the dead lake, was a hunting camp. Neither were in danger of being spotted as the sun rose behind them.

Ksenia had chosen a practical outfit. She delighted in wearing dresses made from extravagant feathers from species in her sanctuary. This one was woven of feathers from chameleonic dragons; thus, her attire reflected the scorched reds of the environment. Alejandro wore his orange leviathan-leather scarf, and a faded blue linen tunic, over which was smoky grey leather armour.

Pikes surrounded the camp, deterring anything from attacking. Sentries leaned lazily by a few. Pointed tents, spacious and airy, in camouflaged patterns of baked red and forest green filled the interior.

One thing, impossible to miss, was the huntress, posing in splendour, straddling the body of a velothdraig. As if being brought down for someone's ego wasn't grotesque enough, the fifteen-metre-long dragon had this gloating monstrosity upon it, her portrait being painted. Violet scaled skin around the eyes and jaws diffused into dark amber, before meeting a crown of ivory horns. In death it looked more in subjugation, than peace.

Ksenia spoke bitterly, "Those scum have taken a veloth! Gods, it's no wonder she wants a mirrored draig. To have her own image reflected from the animal whilst she kills it! She's wants one to serve as a mirror!"

Ksenia's blood boiled. She felt as though she might charge the camp and begin hacking. Alejandro placed a hand gently on her shoulder, with a surprisingly cold touch. Ksenia was clueless as to how he curbed his temper.

"We'll avenge it, Ksenia, hold your temper. Think of it like bringing a bow to full draw," Alejandro continued, looking through his monocular. "You have to gather force, stretch the right muscles until you reach your anchor point. Otherwise, your shot is weak."

As much sense as that made to Ksenia, it didn't abate her temper. Ksenia was eager to put this wretch out of action, for good.

The huntress was Logh Hedrin, a Reywhern and Castle member. The Republic of Reywher was far off, on the north-western point of The Sigel. It was common knowledge, even as far as The Mane, that nobody liked Reywherns.

Reywher was divided between polarised political extremes, with one government in the south representing far left ideals and one on the north representing far right ideals, and no outsider could tell the difference. Famed for obnoxiousness, ignorance, and war mongers, they made poor neighbours.

Hedrin was tall, lean, and clearly athletic. She looked in her mid-forties, with golden hair tied up in gilded talons. Her face was angular, and her eyes bright blue.

"They'll have chariots," Alejandro continued. "Hedrin is famed for chasing down prey with hounds."

Ksenia was shocked by Alejandro's knowledge of Castle members. He had to have profiles on most of them, and when she had asked, all he said was, "I have a guy in Wetsven."

Wetsven was a large, painfully wealthy country on The Sigel. It held a neutral status in all affairs, by holding everyone's wealth, treasures, and secrets in the most secure vaults known. It also provided a home for the Flint Castle.

Ksenia had replied, "Probably the same guy I have." Her spy was an Archery Guild member who she gave exotic feathers to in return for information.

"That arquebus," Alejandro went on, still looking through his lens. "ARQ-VI, gilded to high Anordaithe, but I'd guess she's also a part of the Powder Masters. You know that cult?"

Despite having never heard of it, Ksenia's blood froze. "Cult?"

"Far right, religious fundamentalists who believe the arquebus is *divine*, the knowledge of its workings given to their founder by their god himself."

"And not invented by a dwarven weaponsmith last century..." Ksenia scoffed.

"How do you confuse a Reywhern?"

She gave him a thoughtful look.

"Use logic."

"Don't many places revere the bow?" Ksenia asked. "The Maytoni, Hasjin... Chanjion – they're Sigel nations too."

"*Revere*, yes. Maytoni see the bow as something of divine significance, due to its use in their myths. The Hasjin, were given a bow by a demigod, who promised that if they held archery first, their dynasty would never fall. Which by the way, it hasn't. And the Chanjion don't revere the bow, so much as respect what it has done for them. It lifted the Tevller occupation from them. But none of them have an unhealthy obsession for bows – and none of them are war mongers."

How Alejandro had such worldly knowledge, Ksenia didn't know. She had never truly left The Mane. Her home was still at least a third 'undiscovered', so there was no need for her to explore other places.

"This Hedrin, she's obviously in better physical shape than I am. A hunter, skilled with ballistics and to make it worse, a religious extremist, who thinks trophy hunting is a divine right."

Once, Ksenia had stumbled upon a mother marsh draig, the fifteen-metre-long beast seemingly sculpted from gleaming, jagged jade. Its blood red eyes were enough to stop a person's heart, yet Ksenia had stared it down, managing a cautious withdrawal. Dragons she knew, but this predator was entirely unnatural; death was her persona.

"I have a plan," Alejandro concluded.

At dusk, Alejandro led her into denser land. He had hidden a raft by the edge of the Ruthvane; the only substantial water source in the region.

Ksenia gingerly made her way through the mini-rain forest. Every low branch armed with thorns caught her hair, whilst Alejandro bounded through this world, which seemed to open before him.

The raft was just as Ksenia had feared; a flat, wide platform of woven lengths of wood. Hardly the pleasure craft she, a former pirate, was expecting. To her relief, Alejandro rowed.

Since their reconnaissance, Ksenia's blood had cooled. Something about the moonlit sailing was gradually caressing the pain and anger from her spirit. When they set off, the flicker of a sandy coloured tail whipped at the surface. Neither of them knew what it was, but it was a wicked flutter of beauty, slowing their hearts.

Morning came with ethereal light, perking up body and soul. Despite the rough conditions, Ksenia was now feeling invigorated. Birds were making themselves known with various calls - she could identify them all.

She pulled herself up and padded back to the ragged walkway on the wall where Alejandro sat, legs crossed, monocle raised.

The ruins had once been a waystation for fishing. Rotten pillars jutted from the water like broken fangs. Walls of vines, with ivy and colourful flowers, ran parallel to each other, the stonework completely consumed. The old guard wall stood seven feet tall, every crack home to toxic forms of ivy and thorny flowering plants.

"Here they are," Alejandro said, keeping his monocle on the far horizon. Ksenia dropped to a knee, careful not to let her skin touch the slithering vines.

"Charging on chariots," she said, taking in the scene. Blurred outlines resembling chariots, raced forward among a storm of dust. "Four chariots, three dogs to each and what, three to four hunters a chariot?"

"Twelve to sixteen arquebuses. And the handlers of those beasts too. You can see them hanging off the back." Ksenia could just make out the bulk of each figure, clutching a lengthy whip.

"Ten to one, at the very least," Ksenia muttered, as the details of the charge came into view. Now, her blood was simmering again.

"Hang on a moment..." Alejandro sounded unsure. A jolt of worry burst within Ksenia's stomach.

"What is it?"

"They do have bows. Look."

As the horde slowed to a halt, Ksenia watched several hunters jump from the chariots, longbows in hand.

"There's no way she'll want to slay this draig with a bow..." Ksenia whispered.

Then, they saw the means behind the bows.

Twelve of the sixteen hunters stood in a semicircle behind the chariots and raised their longbows high. The cumbersome piles of the arrows were visible even a hundred yards off.

"Whistling arrows?" Alejandro ventured.

"No, something worse..." Ksenia watched the hunters loose the arrows into the sky. Silence followed, but the hounds tied to the chariots turned feral, howling distressingly, and thrashing against their bonds. Their handlers instantly set upon them with whips.

"Shrieking arrows," Ksenia answered disparagingly. "Set to deliver a shriek only draigs – and other animals can hear."

Over the tumult came a raging wail of pure anger. The dogs fell silent, frozen in trepidation and Ksenia thought she even saw the hunters quivering. By contrast, Ksenia's heart fluttered, a flush of hot excitement poured up over her neck and face.

"How acute is the pitch?" Alejandro asked.

"Extreme, enough to draw out the animal – it can even stun the draig, bring it crashing to the ground," Ksenia hissed venomously. "That's how they're going to kill it!"

"Get ready, Ksenia..." Alejandro put his monocle away and picked up his exquisite bow. He adjusted the glove over his left hand with his teeth.

"You're forgetting I used to be a pirate, right?" She eagerly pulled up her own bow, the feathered sculpting complimented with vivid blue bars along the limbs. Internally she was screaming at Alejandro to start the ambush.

Another roar, this one more fury than pain, struck their ears.

Alejandro had a regular arrow nocked, not wishing to obliterate any life residing within the environment. With such dryness, the arid land would fuel the fury of the flames until there was nothing left. Rather, these arrows held blue and green bared flights, fletched from a rain griffin's feathers with the shafts dyed deep ruby from dragon's blood. Whilst griffin feathers were famed for giving the arrow a truer flight, dragon's blood would increase the resiliency of the shaft tenfold.

With the exception of the griffin feathers, Ksenia's arrows were the same, though she preferred draig feathers, for the faster speed they provided. There was a golden sheen with iridescent undertones of bronze through her flights.

"I've an idea, but it's hardly the restrained notion of an ambush," Alejandro began, pulling his regular arrow off the string, replacing it with a phoenix arrow. He pulled his protective scarf over the lower part of his face and leapt from the wall, bolting into the open.

Ksenia stumbled to her feet, looking off to the left as something stole her attention. The mirrored reflection of the harsh world swirled into the sky, with glints of emerald and swaths of rust. Ridges of gleaming, sparkling spines ran along an uneven back, with small wings formed by crystal-like webbing and pinions of clear feathers. Two smaller, thicker, legs at the front held the gait of the beast, whilst the rear legs were leaner and built for propelling it forward or into the air.

She was utterly lost by the exquisite sight; the wonder of nature's artistry twirled upwards, the colours of the world rolling from its sleek form. To her, it was indisputably the most beautiful feeling one could experience, deep in their soul.

Then, like an all-consuming abyss, came the reality of the situation before her. Despite the heat of the phoenix arrows, the fleeing draig could still be felled from the sky by the paralysing anguish delivered through the shrieking arrows.

As the next volley went up, Ksenia saw Alejandro loose his arrow into the air to meet it.

Just what in Anordaithe is he doing?

At the peak of the arc, Alejandro's arrow struck the hunter's volley and the whole world plummeted into midnight. Then, from the point of impact bloomed wave after wave of flame, so vivid it seemed to pull in all darkness from the surrounding area. The wild plumes exuded an unquenchable fury, seeming to echo the very wrath of a phoenix.

Gods, Ksenia thought, *it probably is!*

The world around her became even wilder, as every living creature let loose cries of panic. Jagged ridges ripped through ferns behind Ksenia, and over them stampeded a dozen tall, flightless birds. Foliage all about Ksenia exploded with life, a frightening revelation of just how close they were at any one time to such dangerous snakes, insects, and lizards.

Everything brightened again as the fire clinging to the sky folded in on itself, to a single centre point, taking the last streaks of darkness with it.

Ksenia's ears rang in the wake of the fire's dissipation. Focus returned to her, and the hunters, splayed over the ground, were getting to their feet. Hedrin was barking orders.

At the same moment as Hedrin, Ksenia noticed just how exposed Alejandro was. Ksenia cried at him to run as he turned. A bark from Hedrin's arquebus, muffled by distance, broke over the landscape. Alejandro grunted, flinching as he bounded back to cover.

The other hunters had tossed aside their longbows, with arquebuses aimed towards Alejandro – and her.

Alejandro tore through the only entry in the wall and clambered back up the walkway.

"Something just occurred to me," Alejandro panted, clutching his right thigh. Before he could continue, there was a chorus of blasts. Explosions in the foliage whooshed by them.

"What?" Ksenia replied, brushing twigs and leaves away. Another snap and whizz hit her ears at the same time debris from the wall struck her face like raking claws. She snarled at the streak of hot pain.

"Those black-power ballistics are a fire hazard." Alejandro rose and loosed an arrow as the cover of branches around him was ripped apart.

"Oh, they're the fire hazard?" Kesnia snapped, eyes bright and demanding answers.

"I'm not a military strategist, but I feel we should have been better prepared."

"Look, wildfires are necessary, otherwise there's too much growth. If that happens, then, _when_ something does catch fire, the blaze becomes a firestorm and consumes far more than it should. Animals can go extinct, habitats are obliterated, and what's affected can never completely recover – it's just as devastating as any of these Castle twats!"

More volleys crashed over their heads and ripped stone from their cover. Alejandro was hunched down, looking at her intently.

"You're right, though. The draigs, their fire breathing, functions as a natural part of cleaning out these lands. But it's done seasonally, _gradually_, through disputes over mates and territory. Here and now, with arquebuses, there's the potential to devastate this entire landscape with a stray ember!"

"Well, let's put them down fast," Alejandro shouted over the tumult of roaring arquebuses, though Ksenia knew it was not going to be that simple.

"They're moving up, Alejandro," she panted, daring a look over the wall. Sucking in a deep breath, Ksenia rose and loosed an arrow at the front runner. The hunter took the arrow high in the chest and tumbled. Alejandro, with a regular arrow, managed to strike another, before a volley forced them back to cover. Ksenia was about to rise again as they reloaded, however razor shards of debris struck her face as a second volley roared.

"Timed volleys," she hissed. "We need to move out of here before they flank us."

"Follow me," Alejandro said.

The pair charged into the jungle; all vivid light lost to inky shade. A volley of shots ripped through the foliage behind them. Ksenia yelped, feeling the torrent of air close to her exposed arms. Cries from the hunters rose up. Worse, the voices were close.

Two metres ahead, Alejandro braced himself by a grey-barked tree and loosed an arrow, with a sharp cry following it. She looked to Alejandro. If he was tense, it didn't show. He looked beyond her, signalling for Ksenia to turn. As she did, she made out the silhouette of a hunter and drew her bow, loosing quickly. As the arrow struck the hunter, Alejandro charged past her and snatched the arquebus from the man's hands.

He closed his left hand, dead to all feeling, over the cord on the top of the weapon, smothering it and any risk of fire. As more commotion rose around them, Alejandro set the weapon down gently and nodded knowingly. Ksenia understood. She turned to the closest noise and drew on the figure among the foliage. As she loosed the arrow, Alejandro rushed by. He snatched the arquebus from the hunter and smothered the fuse, before ducking back into the cover of another tree.

In this way, they dispatched another six, the thick confines of the jungle keeping them hidden.

"That's it then!" A voice called out. "My entourage is dead or fleeing."

"Oh, please don't tell me she's going to play the victim..." Ksenia panted, leaning against coarse bark, as Alejandro hid behind another. His bow was held against his chest, ready.

"I've pulled gracious victories from setbacks worse than this!" Hedrin cried out again. "You hardly burn bright enough for a phoenix!"

"Oh, of course, you get all the attention," Ksenia whispered, giving the man a knowing look. A shoulder shrug was the only reply.

"Divine fire comes from the steel of our weapons! Not your false god!" Hedrin continued.

"Please not a sermon..." Ksenia groaned.

A deafening crack sounded with a force so intense, all breath was stolen from Ksenia. In an instant, the world became night and she felt buried alive, before realising that she had collapsed under the foliage.

Ksenia couldn't move, feeling blood wetting her ears and tasting it in her mouth, as she lay there.

Salvation came in the form of Alejandro, as he pulled her to her feet. The world spun, tilting one way, then the other. It took a moment for Ksenia to realise her hearing had been impaired. Alejandro's face was all she could see. He ran his eyes over her with a meticulous gaze, looking for wounds.

"You're okay," he said, though his voice was coming through like the remnants of an echo. "She's got grenades. Stay here," he said, moving away.

Ksenia decided that she would be damned if she was going to hang back. Gracelessly, she staggered after him. Alejandro ducked to the right in cover from something unseen ahead, and Ksenia ducked to the left, mirroring him. She saw him burst out again; bow drawn. He loosed an arrow into the blinding white light before charging after it. Eyes straining with moisture, Ksenia hammered after him, every gnarled root threatening to trip her. The world formed about her as she entered the clearing and the cries of both Alejandro and Hedrin rose up slowly, until her ears popped.

By the cover of a fallen log, Alejandro lay. The huntress was only fifteen metres off, her gaudy weapon held in one hand, whilst she used the cord to ignite the fuse on another grenade.

Ksenia didn't hesitate and drew on Hedrin. In her fugue state, however, she forgot to nock an arrow, noting this error at the last minute. Through the power of sheer panic, Ksenia grasped her dagger and with no grace or poise, launched it at the huntress to stall for time.

Alejandro rose, loosing his own arrow, striking the huntress in the upper torso. Hedrin barked in bitter irritation, dropping to one knee as her ARQ-VI fell to the dusty ground, clattering noisily. The grenade hit the dirt with a dull thud next to her.

Ksenia was ready this time, throwing her arms over her head and dropping into a crouch.

The abrupt crunch was more severe, as Hedrin's own store of powder went up with the explosion. The world under her shuddered as if a comet had come crashing from the sky.

In the sudden silence descending over them, the first thing Ksenia heard was, "Not even enough left for a funeral portrait." She unwrapped her arms from around her head. A guttural sigh of exertion came from Alejandro, as he fell back to rest on the fallen log.

A glint caught Ksenia's eye, something almost under her periphery. She looked down to see a gleaming, silver feather caught on the buckle of her belt.

Travel from The Sigel was simple. Though Luci hated ships, Orion's company galleon was furnished to the point where she forgot she was on one.

Arriving in Bravenasil there were three signs which could have led to the Phoenix Archer: Trevor Geddenson, who was hunting cassowary in the northeast; Jany Smith, bow-hunting bears in the west; Loch Hedrin, looking for a new species in the northwest. All of them, missing.

Orion was unperturbed with where to begin, his patience preternatural.

After an inquiry through the Wetsven embassy, they discovered Trevor Geddenson was dead, beaten to death by a mob of kangaroos. Luci cackled at the news. She adored kangaroos, considering them the most genteel of thugs in the natural world.

Smith had disappeared in a region of forest so dense that the mountain peak within it was considered impossible to reach. That was all Luci needed to know.

Finally came Hedrin.

The guard nodded towards the cell. He wore a resplendent uniform of ruby and ebony which contrasted against the bleak surroundings.

Slumped in the cell was one of Hedrin's entourage, caked in dirt and filth. Age was impossible to discern through the grime, and the haggard hair and beard were matted down with grease.

Luci nodded their thanks as Ori approached the bars. He placed an arm high up, leaning against them and gave a casual whistle. From the dank, the prisoner lifted his head, squinting at them suspiciously.

"Logh Hedrin," Ori began. "You were a member of her hunting party, eh?"

The prisoner sat there, sullen.

"What are you? Mercenary? Pirate? Or just a hanger-on, looking for gold?"

The prisoner said nothing.

"Why was he pulled in?" Luci asked the guard.

"We caught him selling powdered panther talons as a 'cure-all'," the guard replied, with a voice as cold as the cells.

"The Castle frowns on that," Luci muttered, rubbing a hand over her mouth and chin.

Orion gave the guard a dark look. The guard moved to unlock the cell. "Go ahead. They leave their rights at the door."

Stalking forwards, Ori leaned down, took the man by the throat, and rammed him against the wall. "Logh! Hedrin! What happened to her!?"

"Get me out of here, then I'll tell you." The prisoner gasped, hands feebly pawing at Orion's wrist.

"Do you know the ruination you inflict, selling lies?" Orion snapped; teeth bared. "The harm you inflict, condemning people to a fate worse than death; flogging false hope?"

The guard was standing with his back turned to the cell, looking out of a barred window indifferently.

"Answer my question," Orion growled.

"It was a phoenix, okay! No one believes me!"

Ori put his fist into the man's gut like a battering ram. The prisoner slumped against the wall.

"What's the mark for his crime?" Luci asked the guard who was still pondering the outside world.

"We cut off the lips; show the world the wickedness behind a con-artist's smile."

Luci gave a look to Orion and the Chief pulled his flaying knife from its sheath.

"He's *actually* here. In The Mane, in Bravenasil," Orion spoke, clapping his hands sharply, as they left the jail.

There was something uplifting about finally catching wind of elusive prey. Something which washed away fatigue or despair and push a hunter on further. A reinvigoration deep within the soul.

"The world isn't so big anymore, is it?" Luci added, a tad forlorn. "What happens when it's all known and trodden over?"

"Nature will never let us win, Luci," Orion replied matter-of-factly as they moved out. The street was wide, ordained by numerous displays of wildflowers alive with bees and butterflies, bracketed by affluent taverns and merchants.

"I'd hope not. Otherwise, what are we to do? Start killing each other until no one is left?"

"There will always be something, Luci. Nature is eternal, and will adapt and throw challenges our way until, like you said, there are none of us left."

"You make it sound like it's a losing battle. If the Committee knew this, there'd be a rebellion." Luci was teasing, but she knew how affronted the Castle members would get at this personal philosophy.

"Nature's the mightiest power in the universe and allows us to challenge it. What Nature provides is a never-ending struggle which allows people like us to rise to our full potential. And we will."

Part II – The Fluted Deer

"Why in Anordaithe would you sneak into my bedchamber?" Alejandro Zaragosa sighed gruffly, sitting upright in bed.

At the chamber's entrance stood Ksenia Kiamount, holding onto the hunched figure of Blair Ruthvane. From his chest, Blair, wincing and biting into his upper lip, gingerly removed a flint dagger.

"We should've waited till morning," Ksenia sighed, taking the dagger from Blair as the man composed himself.

Blair strutted forward; his other hand extended in greeting as if none of this was peculiar in any way. "No matter. Mister Zaragosa, a pleasure, nonetheless."

"Alejandro, let me explain. Honestly, there's a... *reason* for this," Ksenia attempted, though she knew the explanation was no less strange.

"Blair Ruthvane," he repeated, hand still extended.

Alejandro sat at the edge of the bed. He looked to the hand, then Blair. Then, with a perplexity Ksenia had never seen on a face, he looked at her, before looking back to Blair.

"You're looking well," Alejandro responded. "For someone two-hundred-years dead."

"I opened a bottle of Krewth, in anticipation," Blair said, pulling a chair back for Ksenia.

"Such foresight," Alejandro replied sardonically. He took a seat at his marble table, its white veins silver under the moonlight. He was wearing only breeches. Ksenia hadn't known the extent of his scaring. Like lightening, jagged bolts stabbed down Alejandro's left side.

"Ksenia informed me of your wine cellar, but I saw this on the way in, and thought it sufficient." Blair poured for Ksenia. She gave Alejandro an apologetic look, getting a flat stare back.

"At least the cellar was saved." Alejandro took the offered bottle and poured himself plenty.

"First, we toast. You don't open a bottle of Krewth without first toasting the host – it's bad luck."

"Is it now."

"To Alejandro!" Ksenia intervened. "A man who places others before himself."

She, with Blair, raised their goblets.

Weary eyed with a warm grin, Blair had finely maintained silvery stubble over his ruddy skin. His dark auburn hair, on the other hand, was dishevelled, coming down to his neck. In appearance, Ruthvane was a paradox, looking both neat and untidy simultaneously.

"Quite a homestead. I like how cosy it is," Blair rambled on. Of course, Ksenia knew what 'cosy' meant: small.

"Yes, never a problem to keep heated..." Alejandro retorted. "How are you here?" He demanded, leaning forward.

"Well, I met Lady Kiamount outside town – rather fortunate – as I was passing through on my way to her sanctuary."

"No... I meant, *how*, are you, at two hundred years dead... at my table, drinking my Krewth?"

"Ah! I forget this is unusual. First, I've been dead one hundred and ninety-seven years, and it's a boringly obvious answer, but I am in fact, a vampire."

Ksenia knew what was coming and jumped in first. "Just listen, Alejandro."

"I've always been troubled – Lady Kiamount, I am sorry you have to hear this again – that is, by my family's legacy. Imagine being born with a conscience, into a family immune to such."

"But you're the heir to the greatest exploration dynasty. Ruthvane is a name known throughout the world. Lakes, mountains, even regions, are named after your family," Alejandro replied, perplexed more by the revulsion Blair held for his family than having been forced into entertaining a vampire in the middle of the night.

"No one mentions I'm related to the man who founded the Expeditionists in the Dytrentian army, now the greatest thieves known. Or that my great-grandfather helped the Dytrentians cross the Ferg River, leading to the genocide of Ahkali. Or that my father explored the jungles of The Mane, killing any tribe in his path, looting whatever looked worth something. The Cerulean Plague? Also, my father. When delving into untouched territories here, he brought the virus with him." Blair paused to let a forlorn breath escape, then took a swing of the wine. "These are only a few of the ugly truths of the name I bear."

Silence followed, and Ksenia felt the potent pang of sympathy she had when Blair first told her this. She knew how lucky she was by comparison. Her family had protected and studied the natural world, never at its expense. As she looked at the long dead explorer, she saw how Blair and herself were in essence, two sides of the same coin, representing civilisation.

"Well-" Alejandro began.

"You're going to give an example of something positive my family has done, aren't you?" Blair cut in like a whip.

Alejandro fell silent.

"Sorry. I know, we Ruthvanes are pioneers of the natural world!" Now, Blair sounded truly forlorn. "We were pirates at best... Oh, no offense, Lady Kiamount," he stammered, placing an apologetic hand on her forearm.

"Youthful rebellion," Ksenia added, unoffended.

"I know you pillaged the wealthy to fund your family's sanctuary, so it's not quite the same in my eyes."

"I'm sorry, Blair, really," Alejandro added. "We could all learn a great deal from you. So why the... Disappearance?"

Blair waved a hand. "Oh, it's not complicated at all. I never intended to wander off into the wild and let nature take me. I sought out the Plague Queen. She's real."

A grim silence fell over the table.

The myth of the Plague Queen was ominous. It told of a mage of renowned power, devoted to understanding every plague and sickness known. Within Anordaithe it was understood that the more magical knowledge acquired, the more a person's sanity was eroded. And yet somehow, the Plague Queen was immune to this.

"After I explained my plight, she granted me vampirism. I wanted the Ruthvane plague to end with me, yet I was compelled to do as much good as I could. And, after *much* thought, I decided on vampirism," Blair concluded.

"I don't want to poke holes in your plan," Alejandro interjected, a placating hand raised. "Especially since you're committed to it at this point. However, vampires are undead, and only... exist through the consumption of blood: human, dwarf, centaur... any of *us*."

"Give me some credit. I said I thought it through. There is after all, no shortage of bad people in the world."

"So, cannibalism was preferable to being a Ruthvane, is what I'm hearing..." Alejandro said, raising an eyebrow.

"Don't be so narrow minded."

"Ksenia, help me out. I never thought I'd be justifying the morality of cannibalism."

"It's drinking blood. I'm not roasting anyone on a spit!" Blair retorted.

"Okay!" Ksenia exclaimed, arms held out, freezing both men mid-argument. "Blair, tell him why you're here."

The world was a kaleidoscope of wonder for Ksenia. Wonder being the baseline. Deviation from this was either sinister, or weird. Blair Ruthvane's return was both.

Ksenia had never met a vampire before – that she knew of. Blair was a first. She hardly knew what to say, other than the instinctual pleading for a donation to keep her sanctuary running. Now, several days later, her image of the Ruthvanes had been spun on its axis.

Ruthvane's problem was enough to make her blood boil – which, she admitted, wasn't overly difficult.

A century ago, a group of Crown nations went to war, and in doing so, almost wiped out their populations of fluted deer through the violence. Fluted deer were famed for the furrowed holes within their antlers; each shake or clash of heads produced a melodious chorus.

Surviving deer were moved into The Mane, placed in temperate environments. Despite these efforts, they never fully recovered.

As if the deer had not been persecuted enough, the Flint Castle wanted a large number of them. Specifically, Narfi Bailey. The man was the Castle's most ambitious expansionist. Unsatisfied with a lodge situated in The Sigel, Narfi wanted one on every continent. Orion Aldenberg was willing to realise Narfi's ideals and asked him to establish a lodge in The Crown, thus Narfi wanted the heads of many of The Crown's famed species to sing in constant chorus around it.

Keeping the animals safe was a crusade for Blair, having originally come from The Crown. Bringing the deer back from the brink of extinction was a penance.

Yet the first large problem to overcome was Blair's nature. A giveaway that someone was a vampire was the lack of animals – any animals – present. On some level, animals sensed the aura of death, instinctively fleeing.

Assurances were given and Blair produced a pendant shaped like a rat, the insignia of the Ruthvane family. The metal had been taken, allegedly, from the mythical dwarven city of Golmethin, said to exist inside a mountain under the deepest ocean. It retained the ability to absorb any darkness around the wearer, permitting social camouflage. When the horses at the stable didn't flee, Ksenia was reassured.

Though, a carriage was required, given Blair's aversion to sunlight.

Towards the end of their journey, Ksenia felt the carriage halt. Within was Blair, catching as much sleep as he could.

From outside came a voice, its coherence filtered out by the padding of the carriage. Then came Alejandro's unmistakable iron tone. Ksenia felt sparks in her veins, enough to make her jump from the carriage, a hand over her curved emerald blade. It was dark enough for Blair to safely follow, though he did warily.

Instantly, Ksenia met the figure of Alejandro, having jumped from the top of the carriage. He too had a hand over his own dagger and turned to face the single rider blocking the road.

"Well met, sir," Alejandro began, stalking forward. Ksenia kept up as Blair stayed by the horses. Fifty metres ahead was a man astride a horse, the animal turned to block the road with its size. This figure was every part the knight of a royalist state. His plate armour was layered, gold in colour with forest green trimming, enforcing a formidability which froze Ksenia for a moment.

It was hardly Narfi, Ksenia thought. However, the colours and uniform were unmistakably Formardin, the state from which Narfi came.

"The Lord of the Formardin Cometeers, Narfi Bailey, wishes to extend an invitation to meet him on the jousting field," the rider shouted.

"To the point. Good. I'm wrecked and want to bed down with some wine," Ksenia add through an impatient sigh.

Ignoring her, the rider continued. "You are the one known as The Phoenix Archer?"

With a half-grin, his scars bared to the world, Alejandro replied, "What makes you think that's me? We're just humble brigands, looking for a bit of sheep rustling."

"Lord Bailey is aware of your presence and has asked that you resolve any animosity in a *principled* fashion," the rider continued.

Ksenia did not believe for one minute that they had a choice, though she was certain the rider was alone.

"What, my bow against his sword?" Alejandro looked to Ksenia, "Sounds fair to me."

"I'll second the *honourable* Phoenix Archer," she mocked.

There was silence with the rider giving nothing away. His horse looked bored. The rider pulled the animal around, with a snort of annoyance coming from it, and trotted forwards. Ksenia's hand fell back to her dagger, and she was ready – and hoping – for a fight. This noble blustering, and pre-arranging of killing was nonsense. Just another way for the social elite to think themselves better than commoners, despite falling to the same base desires for violence.

The rider extended a hand with parchment in it, leaning down for Alejandro to take it.

Ksenia was disappointed he didn't pull the twat from his saddle for a laugh.

To Ksenia's disbelief, Alejandro then said, "Tell Narfi I shall meet him."

The Tilscasian region was uninhabited, forested, with a semi-circle of mountains to the south-west, the base of them meeting a crescent shaped lake.

"Even the females have antlers," Ksenia breathed quietly, in awe.

The deer stood ten feet tall on hooves of bronze, supporting black antlers sweeping back along their bodies, gleaming with the intensity of a lightning strike. Against the indigo shades of the forest, white streaks over the fur glowed ethereally, with silver eyes gleaming in the darkness.

"They are ancient." Blair whispered.

"By who's standards?" Alejandro quipped.

The vampire stifled a laugh. "I mean, long before most other species of deer we know came about, these were already carrying their song of being around the world."

Now night, the beasts had bedded down. With no breeze, only the occasional turn of a head left a gentle musical note hanging over the forest.

Since encountering the emissary, they had spent a further day traveling before arriving in the region. Ksenia was mortified by the invitation for a duel and stunned further by Alejandro's decision to accept.

"There are two ways to disarm a bear-trap," Blair had said. "One is to throw a rock at the spring, the other is to stick your boot into it." Ksenia had felt hopeful with Blair on her side - before he ruined things. "But I'd be honoured to stand as your second," he finished.

"This is the best option we have to protect the deer," Alejandro affirmed. "That herd is at least one hundred in number. We can't sit around waiting for Nafri to strike, and I won't use the animals as bait either. Just because he thinks himself honourable, does not mean that we must delude ourselves too."

"Honour's a joke," Ksenia added, bitterly. "Just a façade to ensure a fight is fixed to play to someone's strengths."

"And I'm hoping he thinks we'll humour his so-called honour. Remember, Ksenia, we're archers: rogues, miscreants, scum." Alejandro gave a half-smirk. "I know exactly how to beat him."

Morning came, with the golden disc of the sun peeking above the horizon. A concert was already in full force, filling the natural world. Bird's songs, rodent's cries, and howls from wolves and wild dogs were lost to the melody.

On horseback, they made their way to Narfi's camp. Blair was wearing a hood, leather gloves, and a copper mask; his cover that of a rot plague survivor, and thus disfigured. The hood and mask were a contrast to his formal attire, a rich burgundy vest and charcoal grey tunic and breeches.

Nobility made her sick, Ksenia thought. Out here in the wilds, they still insisted on the opulence of home. A dozen tents, each larger than the average family's cottage, were clustered together, tapered upwards to a point. The sheen of the material reflected the misty blue of a comet's trail, reaching higher into warmer colours towards the point of the ceiling. Surrounding the camp were stakes aimed outwards and sentries holding pikes.

"Men-at-arms," Blair explained. "Unbloodied infantry, hence, the colder colours of their mail. Only veterans wear the colours of a blazing comet."

"Is this a hunting camp or a military incursion?" Ksenia gasped.

"Long way from home!" Blair called out to the approaching guard, a giant of man at seven-feet tall, in rich burgundy mail, iridescent with gold.

"Aye, halt there," the guard called back. "What's with the grim façade?" He nodded towards Blair.

"Stared too long into your mother's maw," Ksenia shot back. "Got a bake like a rotting tree trunk."

"He's clearly descended from giants and you're picking a fight with him," Alejandro muttered. "And you rebuked me for being reckless."

"Is it plague? And if so, is it contagious?" The guard went on, ignoring the slight.

"Neither," Ksenia replied. "And none of your business, interloper. I'm not about to face interrogation by trespassers in my own home."

This lean wall of armour was vexing her no end. Already her blood was simmering at the sheer arrogance of being told to halt by a man in her homestead. Ordinarily, this would be sorted by a slash of her dagger up across the face, but she needed to keep her pirate's nature restrained just a short while more.

"Both King and minister bade us welcome. Anyways, Lord Bailey is waiting. I assume one of ye is the grandiose Phoenix we've been told to be wary of," he went on, sounding unimpressed. "My ancestors were giants, and I still have kin in The Maw – twelve foot and more. There's nothing in all Anordaithe we can't kill." He spat into the mud. "A phoenix can die just like anything else. There'll be a way. We just haven't found it yet."

Alejandro gave a dark half-smirk as he moved his horse past the giant. Ksenia and Blair followed his lead. Despite being the enemy here, the pike soldiers yielded to their path, though they seemed to form a corridor, steering them in a specific direction.

The din of metal and exploding wood took their attention. The height of the tents was enough to block out the rising sun, and obscure any view of the valley, and so when the trio rounded the last corner, they were surprised to find a jousting field had been carved into the land. One burnt-orange armoured knight was being lifted to his feet by squires in misty attire. Towards their end, a rider pulled his animated steed about to face them. He wore resplendent armour of smouldering gold, with blue-hot lining. The helmet was angular, ornately sculpted flames flecked with diamonds trailing from it.

"My Lord!" the giant shouted from behind them. "Presenting The Phoenix Archer and company."

"Indeed!" The rider, obviously Narfi, hooted as he trotted forward. "I can guess by such grisly scars. Gods, man, haven't you ever considered a scarf." Narfi pulled his faceguard up to reveal hardly a comely visage; dark, shaggy eyebrows, a wide flat nose which had been broken time and time again, and a mouth twisted into a perpetual pout. His skin was pale, though smeared with grime.

"Scars, I find, have good stories behind them," Alejandro replied, unoffended. "They should be worn openly – I can see from your nose; you feel the same way."

Narfi's glare darkened. "Well, thank you for meeting me on an honourable field," he continued, nonetheless.

"Looks like any other field," Alejandro interrupted, testing his opponents' character.

"Ha! To those of a lower station, such as yourselves. But seen through the discerning eye of the well-bred, this jousting field will exalt the best of us."

Ksenia found his tone to be exceedingly patronising.

"This, archer, is where you and I will determine who has rights over these deer." Narfi held out a hand as two squires pulled forward a cart, upon which was the lifeless body of a fluted deer.

Numbness struck Ksenia first, before the empathy which most hunters lacked, snaked through her. A torrent formed around her heart, rising to her throat.

Blair spoke first. "It seems you have broken the terms of this duel already."

"Hardly. These beasts are mine by divine right, as is anything shaped by the Gods. My terms dictate that should you win..." Narfi sneered. "I shall leave them alone. And anyway, it seems the animals aren't without cruel trickery."

With no decorum, the squires shoved the head of the deer back and forth. Only silence followed, then Ksenia laughed.

"In death their charm follows them. Wherever it is we end up in the next life, Narfi, that deer is laughing at you!" Blair chuckled at that, and Alejandro grinned too.

"Well, it makes no difference!" Narfi hissed. "We've begun rounding them up. That elegant chorus isn't coming from the valley; it's coming from the other side of my camp. I shall just have to keep them penned up in the grounds of my new lodge. The Gods are good, and I get what I want."

"Right, well, let's get on with this," Alejandro bristled impatiently. "How are we to do this? Two great big wooden poles, then charge at each other like cavemen?"

"Oh, archer, I am letting you retain that commoner's plaything, whilst I shall take a lance. If you unseat me with an arrow, you win. *When* I unseat you, the deer are mine."

"The deer are nobody's." Alejandro muttered, as he was waved to the nearest side of the lane. Narfi saluted Alejandro mockingly, before turning a trotting off to the far end.

"This game is rigged," Ksenia muttered.

"Of course. Honourable men like Narfi can't stomach losing," Blair muttered. "Alejandro, I implore you, let me ride against him."

"Don't worry," Alejandro began. He removed his bow-quiver and handed it to Ksenia. "Once Narfi is on his back, they'll try to kill us.

Unsheathe the feathers, and the heat will send the penned deer wild."

"They'll break free and come through this camp like a landslide," Ksenia finished. "So why not do it now?"

"We need to make sure Narfi doesn't escape – I'll take care of that, but don't do anything until he's off his horse."

"But *what* about unseating Narfi? That armour of his, even the horse's attire will be seeping with magic, the kind that knocks incoming arrows off course."

"This whole game of his will be his undoing," he added. "Trust me, Ksenia." With a nod, Alejandro trotted off to the jousting lane, worn down to flat, hard dirt from repeated use. At the far end, on Alejandro's right, Narfi was taking an elliptical shield from a squire, whilst hoisting a colossal lance.

A bark from a steward announced the start, and Narfi shot down the lane like the comet upon his coat of arms. Alejandro raced towards him, drawing his bow. The first arrow twanged off an invisible force as Ksenia suspected it would. A second arrow had been nocked after the first and loosed in haste, sent low and disappearing under the torrent ripped up by Narfi's horse. Narfi was on him, and Alejandro ducked, narrowly avoiding the lance, but even Ksenia could feel the swift gale of its swing. She almost gasped but clenched her fist and readied the quiver instead.

The two horses came around, Alejandro now at the far end of the field. With no respite, Narfi charged, and Alejandro loosed another arrow, clipping the wooden fence, the arrow clattering into the dirt again. He fumbled for another arrow and just about managed to shoot it. But Narfi was almost beside him. Alejandro threw himself to one side to avoid getting impaled, his fingers slipping off the string, launching the arrow into the dirt between them.

What is Alejandro doing?

Ksenia was close to screaming. He was a far better, more level-headed archer than this display...

Then she realised *exactly* what he was doing.

As the third bout began, Narfi's steed began to falter, as the once dry dirt, had, in the blink of an eye, become a quagmire. The beast wailed as its legs went, losing traction in the deluge. Alejandro had pulled his steed off to the side to avoid the mud, and Narfi's horse reeled back, his lance thrown high into the air. The knight came down in a graceless clatter of metal and splosh of mud.

"Those are knight's bane arrows!" Blair exclaimed, hooting, and cheering. And indeed, they were, Ksenia saw. Alejandro put up an amateurish show, as he deliberately put arrows into the ground; arrows infused with magical capabilities, able to turn the hardest of ground into a quagmire.

So excited was Ksenia, she almost forgot her role in the last-ditch plan. She pulled the leather from the flights of the arrows and leapt from her own horse as it reared in panic. Blair was on the ground, his sabre drawn and crying out defiance as many soldiers came at him.

The five-to-one-odds became a moot point as the thunder of hooves and maelstrom of antlers engulfed the scene. Blair leapt aside as the soldiers were trampled, lost completely within a landslide upon which the deer rode.

With a yelp, Ksenia found herself lost amid the mayhem, the tumult threatening to push her into unconsciousness, with a shuddering so intense, she thought her eyes would fall from their sockets. Thick clouds of dust engulfed her. A howling soldier, the giant, came at her. She fumbled for her dagger, grappling against the downward strike. She manged to slash at the giant's midriff, where the layered armour's joins met. A cry told her she had hit something, and the giant's resolve weakened, enough for her to shove him back. Brutally, he was lost from sight as several deer ran through him, as if he had been no more than a pile of hay.

Within the tail end of the stampede, Ksenia saw Blair whip around two pike-wielding soldiers, slashing down one and then the other effortlessly. She pulled her bow around and loosed an arrow at a third coming at the man from behind.

Where was Alejandro? She darted around looking frantically for him as the last of the deer sped by, following the maelstrom as it tore up the camp, trampling the interlopers.

Midway down the jousting lanes, Ksenia finally caught sight of Alejandro. Narfi had recovered, though the glorious shine of his armour was marred with muck, and blood gushed from his helm.

He brought up his shield as Alejandro brought up his bow. No matter, Alejandro shot an arrow at only ten metres or so. The magic of course swatted the arrow violently away, however, the attack forced Narfi to remain on a knee, hidden behind the shield.

Ksenia nocked another arrow and was about to draw, when from the corner of her right eye came a dozen fluted deer, their antler's crying out a vengeful chorus so shrill her blood froze, as did her arms. Narfi had just enough time to turn, his vision consumed by gleaming tines. In full armour, he was gored, then hoisted up by the lead deer.

His own dying cries were lost to the howl of this deer as it summoned its herd back.

Days later, aching still, Ksenia and Alejandro returned to his homestead. She was hoping he felt jubilant enough to go down into his cellar a come out with something extravagant, like a Talmak.

Blair, the gentle man of honour he was, had decided to stay close to the herd for some time further. The fluted deer were under his vigil now, and a likely eternal one at that. Ksenia hoped one day he would shake off the burden of his ancestry and recognise that he was not accountable for their actions, and that the name Ruthvane could be reappropriated by him. He was too good a man to carry around a guilt and shame which belonged to others.

As Ksenia hobbled to the porch, where she hoped to spend the rest of the night with a bottle, she came to a dead halt next to Alejandro.

"Terrific, you're back," came a hard voice.

Sat at the table, were a man and women.

"Alejandro Zaragosa, my name is Evander Penrose, of the Maytoni Summiteers. I'm here for your phoenix arrows."

Part III – The Birds of Exodus

"Maytoni," Ksenia said aloud, with inadvertent reverence.

"A pair," the man, Evander Penrose, replied. He was broad, the figure of a sturdy archer, and around thirty-five. Hard, forest-green eyes sat under unkempt blonde hair. He wore a sapphire surcoat and kangaroo leather armour that kept the shoulders and arms free to wield a bow.

"This," Evander continued, "Is Pastoral Ebrill Glace."

He waved a hand to his partner who wore a beaming smile.

"Hello! You must be Ksenia and Alejandro," she spoke with a cheery tone.

"Well, summiteer or not, you're not taking my arrows," Alejandro snapped. "Leave."

The pastoral was unfazed, despite being lost in Alejandro's shadow. Her skin was unblemished, with eyes gleaming like azure skies. She was wearing a violet tunic, silver-grey breeches with sun-yellow trimming and amethyst embossing.

"Evey, we should have given them time to rest." Ebrill clipped him about the head. "We're sorry for intruding, – at least I am."

"I wanted to ambush you," Evander stated.

"Maytoni needs those arrows," Ebrill went on, ignoring Evander.

"Maytoni aren't known for warmongering," Ksenia added. "Why *would* you need them?"

"We don't *need*, need them," Ebrill reiterated. "But we don't want this kind of power left loose."

"So, you'll bury them, with the rest of your secrets, in Wetsven," Alejandro stated flatly.

"I don't know where our secrets are buried, but give us some credit, it sure as Chasm isn't in Wetsven," Evander cut in, standing.

The pastoral was so disarming it was unsettling, but against her temperamental nature, Ksenia refrained from reaching for her dagger.

"And how did you become the self-imposed authority on the matter?" Alejandro inquired.

"I could ask the same of you," Evander retorted.

"And wasn't it your demi-god who started the Wrathfire."

"Common misconception," Ebrill jumped in. "The Maytoni came together two thousand years ago. The Wrathfire happened four thousand years ago. We don't worship Wrath, though he and the others like him are an integral part of our creation story."

With Ksenia's special interest in animals of flight, she knew the tale of the Wrathfire, which occurred in the centre of The Sigel - the obliteration of numerous civilizations. Wrath had become bitter that a corner of creation, the immortality of the phoenixes, was outside of his power, and tried to slay one. After failing, the beasts knew adversity and turned on the world. The centre of The Sigel became The Ashlands, cut off from all directions, from which nobody ever returned. Each of the five continents had an Ashlands, dead civilisations presided over by phoenixes.

"Wait," Ksenia jumped in. "How often do the Maytoni go after people with these feathers? No one ever comes out of the Ashlands, and the few spots in Anordaithe where phoenix reside are the same. Alejandro won't even tell me where he found his arrows."

"It's seldom a problem but look at the power which is there for anyone to seize,"

Evander replied. "It's rare, but every now and again, someone does." He nodded at Alejandro.

"Perhaps I already know, but how did you find out about my arrows?" Alejandro asked.

"I have a man in Wetsven."

"Wait!" Ksenia drew all eyes to her. Alejandro 'has' a man giving him information on Castle members, and she 'has' a man doing the same. "I'm going to throw a pair of initials out here... A, M."

"Oh, did that serpent sell me out!?" Alejandro hissed, hands clutching the back his neck.

"No need for prejudice," Evander countered. "We go way back. And he didn't 'sell you out'. I had questions about a Dytrentian Prince who was vaporised, and he was too out of character when pressed... So, I dug about his study whilst he slept."

"Classy..." Ebrill sighed.

"How do you know Aeker Murdock?" Ksenia asked.

"Given his status in the Archery Guild, he's in a great position to hear anything regarding phoenix feathers. We met about fifteen years ago. I found him washed ashore on the islands of Oakthei – but that's another story."

The group was silent for a moment.

"I keep an eye on Castle members too. If anyone wanted a go at a behemoth, phoenix fletched arrows would be best." He paused, placing a fist on the marble table. "Are you aware that Orion Aldenberg is here?"

"In The Mane?" Alejandro replied coolly, though Ksenia caught the undercurrent of concern.

"In Bravenasil, with Luciana Doran."

Ksenia's stomach rolled, a clash of fear and excitement. Their actions had summoned the chief of the Castle himself.

"The Castle has strict rules. They don't hunt anything that isn't animal," Alejandro muttered.

"Members can defend themselves, and from their point of view, you've thrown the first dig. And Orion, well, he has no military experience that I can find. He's just a game hunter. But I'd hardly want to go toe to toe with him. I imagine we all know his legend," Evander answered.

Ksenia knew Evander was referring to when Orion slew a behemoth by leaping into its maw and cutting his way to its heart.

"Does *he* want the arrows?" she asked.

"I wouldn't say so. I mean, it doesn't fit with Orion's nature. He likes to be challenged, to have a challenge," Evander replied. "We don't have much on him. I can't find out where he originally comes from. But he joined the Castle eighteen years ago, working through the ranks the old-fashioned way; by merit."

"Thank you for the warning. But my arrows stay with me." Alejandro folded his arms.

Both men fell silent, neither budging.

The events of the last few days suddenly caught up with Ksenia, now needing a bed. Thankfully, Ebrill spoke up with the kind of voice that could stop an army.

"Boys, behave! We're tired, some of us more than others. We can sort this out another time. Besides, Evey and I have another task, and I don't see why you both can't help."

Rain was the most soothing sound Ksenia knew.

The group sat sheltered, under an overhang of rock.

"Arch griffin feathers are best, I find. They're waterproof," Evander was saying. His knowledge in all areas of archery lived up to the Maytoni reputation. From five, all Maytoni began archery in school, continuing until eighteen.

Ebrill had presented their case, "I'll start at the beginning. Maytoni is a word from a long dead language. 'Everyone' is its literal translation." She spoke without any notion of what it was to be patronising, explaining everything in a gentle, knowledgeable manner. It put Ksenia at ease.

"Our people spent fifty years in exodus looking for a home. During this time, numerous other peoples joined, and so the Maytoni grew and eventually we found ourselves in The Sigel next to the Poet's Sea. Whilst our history details events, and of course moral lessons, it doesn't mention where we started."

"I argue it hardly matters," Evander added. "We'd been told to leave."

"Aren't you curious?" Alejandro had said, sitting far easier now. "My ancestors came from The Scar. And one day I'd like to get out there."

Ksenia knew Alejandro was now entranced with their story and enjoying their history lesson. The man was a student of the world, and always curious about people and culture.

Ebrill continued, "Three quarters of Maytoni are descendants from the many peoples who joined the exodus after it began. They know *their* origins on a personal level; my ancestors were nomads from The Crown. Evey's were the Rusenatheans." She explained, referring to the infamous sea-riders.

"That explains the caveman brow," Alejandro jested.

"You're dousing me in wine, I'll let you have that." Evander gave a flirtatious wink.

"We have clues," Ebrill continued. "Arrows, from the first days of the exodus. If we can match the feathers of the arrows to a species, we can narrow things down, and we've heard there may be a flying beast out here to match them."

At this, Ksenia leaned in, taking the bottle, and pouring more wine. "I can help with that. What are the colours?"

The group had ventured into the rainforests of Venai; whole mountains and valleys swallowed up, with ruins of cities lost to time.

"Like clambering into the maw of a tentacled beast," Evander said as they moved out from cover, the rain letting up. "I'm glad I went with the short recurve." Ebrill was unarmed, though Maytoni pastorals were trained in martial arts.

Among thick shadows, the temperature fell, blessedly. Before them were the ruins of temples. Bridges of vines poured from windows, reaching over into other buildings. In the centre was a structure of renown – the largest.

But the world was... _Off_...?

Hosts of kookaburras soared in twisting columns. Mocking, staccato laughter hung over the atmosphere like a tangible force.

"If you flew over on a griffin you wouldn't be able to see this," Ebrill spoke in awe, looking around at the intricate work of vines. "Evey, it's just like the others!"

"The others?" Alejandro said.

"Do you see the distortions in the air, where the birds can only follow specific tracks?" Ebrill began.

Ksenia and Alejandro looked to the streams of kookaburras, the loops drawn with such accuracy by their multitudes. "The Wrathfire was not the first time that Wrath *misbehaved*. When the Gods gave their powers to him and others, Wrath, with Mercy, conspired to keep more people from inheriting this power, thus cultivating a 'demigod' status. The Judge God loosed an arrow between them, and this arrow carved out the Chasm, the bad place where those in love with evil go when they die."

"My creation stories say nothing about a 'bad place'. We don't have one," Ksenia added.

"No bad place?" Evander retorted.

"Well, after this, Mercy and Wrath were marked, so to speak, and if they spent any length of time in one place, their presence would distort the natural world," Ebrill concluded.

"And it wasn't until the Wrathfire that your gods decided that giving us a portion of their power was a bad idea...?" Ksenia added.

"So, this is somewhere Mercy spent time?" Alejandro queried, looking up at the vines and branches, all twisting into one and other. He was grinning with enthusiasm.

"It seems so," Ebrill answered, a squeak of excitement coming from her. "Whereabouts does this bird reside?" She asked, rubbing the sweat from her face with both hands.

"There'll be a shrine up ahead. I'd guess in that main structure," Ksenia replied.

Then Ebrill yelped, a bolt whipping by her; just missing due to Evander pulling her aside. Ksenia and Alejandro clambered over stoney ground to the cover of steps. The kookaburras began shrieking madly.

Alejandro dared a look over the grimy stone, but pulled back, falling into Ksenia as another bolt went by.

"One woman, seventy yards off, crossbow," he spoke rapidly.

Numerous questions needed answering, but Ksenia decided they could wait.

"Ebrill?" She called out, pulling up from cover. Alejandro dragged her down again as a bolt dashed the stonework and spun away with a clang.

"We're okay!" Ebrill cried back.

"We need to get out of here," Alejandro began. "I'll get across to the Maytoni, and you see if you can nail our would-be assassin."

"Oh, the faith you have in me," Ksenia muttered.

Between them and the crossbow-menace, were numerous stoney huts buried under the jungle, providing plenty of cover.

As Ksenia was readying herself to make sure Alejandro wasn't skewered, a shadow bearing the weight of trepidation spread over her. Then came a throaty growl.

The women stalked forward, holding Alejandro's bow, caressing the leviathan leather which kept the heat of the arrows at bay. A mask of watery silver covered her face, as black hair spilled from it. A beige cloak fell from one shoulder, trimmed in pink, half-covering cloudy-bronzed armour. Her figure was built for the fluidity of close quarters fighting; muscular thighs and shoulders but lean enough for speed.

"Talk about serendipity," the woman said. "Here I am, looking to steal prised Maytoni relics, and delivered unto me is the summiteer who destroyed my army, the Phoenix Archer, who it turns out, is real, and the flawless diamond in my crown, the Lady of Feathers!"

"Finally!" Ksenia blurted out. "Someone who knows me. Always in your shadow, Alejandro."

They had been corralled between the intruder's crossbow and her pet, a two-metre tall, blonde minor-griffin in which the only avian features were a pair of magnificent off-white and rose-tinted wings. All were bound at the wrists, on the steps of what had to be the temple, except Evander, who was flat on his back, pinned by a large paw.

Their captor was Slavka Orlov, the *former* commander of the Bloodied Fields Mercenary Company. And, as excited as Ksenia was that Slavka knew who she was, Ksenia could not for the life of her, place her.

"Have we met? I raided so many fat ships back in the day, that all you gaudy twats just run into each other," Ksenia spat.

Slavka stalked across to her and crouched.

"What's with the mask? You can't look worse than it does," Ksenia hissed.

"You cost me a fortune, once," Slavka seethed, her voice coming through the mask like oily smoke. "You're lucky I wasn't aboard, otherwise your little legend would have died there."

"It's outlasted yours," Evander shouted from behind. Slavka shot up, turning.

"I'm glad we've found someone just as mouthy as Ksenia," Alejandro whispered to Ebrill.

"Sorry about this, Alejandro. We honestly didn't expect _her_," Ebrill sighed.

Ebrill had filled them in on Slavka.

A year earlier, brigand forces at the Maytoni and Mundhonnel border unified, and laid siege to Mundhonnel's capital, trapping its army. However, the Maytoni couldn't move a sizable force to the border fast enough. Docked just off the Maytoni waters was Slavka's company who, keenly eyed, offered their services. Maytoni leadership had no choice, and accepted her help, but they managed to negotiate the conflict falling under the supervision of a group of summiteers.

Slavka's company smashed the brigands, and bitter, the remaining forces turned to pillaging the Mundhonnel towns in the south as they retreated, ensuring they got something out of the catastrophe. The summiteers wanted to race around the brigand's flank, blindsiding them and saving the townspeople – except for Slavka, for whom the contract was finished.

Evander led the summiteers in a reckless mission, infiltrating the brigand's camp, assassinating key figures, and setting fire to food and weapon stocks. It was tremendously successful, with the brigands convinced that a larger army was closing in on them. Fleeing east, they crashed into Slavka's company, drunkenly celebrating. This suited the brigands, and they raided, looted and, best of all, took revenge. They demolished the company before dispersing. Maytoni had thought Slavka to be killed in the fighting but learned later she'd escaped.

"Gorgeous cat, what's his name?" Evander was stroking the fur of the leg pinning him. Like all cats, the beast looked somewhere between bored and unimpressed.

"You have become so much chattier since I last saw you," Slavka snapped, standing over him.

"I decided that should I see death coming, I wasn't going out blubbering – I'd smile and laugh."

Ksenia leaned into Ebrill, whispering, "We need a plan."

"Something pragmatic," Alejandro insisted. "She's done a wonderful job with these bonds."

Ebrill's whispered, "Have faith."

"No offense, but I prefer action," Alejandro sighed. "Any knives hidden about you, Ksenia?" Ksenia shook her head and decided to sow small sheaths into her dresses from here on.

"When Evey and I arrived in the capital, he just had to stop and pet every single stray. I'm surprised we ever got through it!" Ebrill called out, stealing Slavka's attention. Slavka whirled and stalked across to her.

"An attack on a Pastoral is a declaration of war with Maytoni, isn't it?" She sneered, the bland stillness of the mask only making the words darker.

"You've already declared war with us. Do your worst," Ebrill snapped.

"I think you'll find your image of the martyr will be far removed from the reality."

"Who said anything about martyrdom?" Ebrill pulled her unbound wrists around and catapulted her brow into the mask, throwing Slavka off balance, before kicking out and destabilising her further.

The lion bellowed, jumping over the body of its master. The pastoral didn't even flinch as the animal came with inches of her.

Evander was up, tackling Slavka as she tried to regain her composure. The lion reared up; Ebrill ducked under it and pulled at the vines covering the stone, tangling its back legs. The beast lost its balance and fell away from the trio, growling bitterly. Ebrill then began untying Alejandro's and Ksenia's bonds.

"Faith, dear archer," she began, softly. "Is having the confidence that the Gods will provide opportunity for action." She gestured to jagged rocks that had been behind her. "It took me a while, but I got there in the end. Fortuitous, Slavka dropped me there, wasn't it?"

Somehow, being outnumbered did nothing faze Slavka. She caught Evander's punch and used his momentum to throw the summiteer into a roll. From out of the air, Slavka summoned her crossbow taking aim at Alejandro. Ebrill threw some form of magical shield between them, and the bolt exploded as it hit it.

Growling, Slavka snatched back the string, a new bolt automatically loading from the magazine.

In the storm of violence, Ksenia found her dagger and rolled low to avoid Slavka's crossbow.

As she leapt up, slashing, Slavka pressed the trigger and a stinging lance bore into Ksenia's stomach. Murky colours swarmed her vision; Alejandro and the others devolving to shapeless blurs as she fell.

She came to slowly, pain and reality ebbing back into her senses.

Ebrill leapt up, hoisting herself on an overhanging outcrop and pulled down the refuse of rock and jungle over the massive, winged cat. The beast growled, batting its gorgeous wings frantically in a futile attempt to take off. Debris battered it to its knees, before the jungle washed over it like a tidal wave, burying it.

Then, Ebrill was leaning down over Ksenia. It was hateful how youthful she looked, Ksenia decided. A burning eruption in her gut had her asking Ebrill's gods for forgiveness at the bitterness.

"I'm stemming the bleeding, and sealing the wound," Ebrill panted, hair matted to her forehead. Ksenia didn't really understand what the pastoral was doing, but assumed it was some form of medical-magic and accepted it.

At the portal to the temple, hot purple energy erupted violently, and Evander and Alejandro dived for cover, clattering down the eroded steps.

"Is she okay?" It was Alejandro, panting, his speech panicked.

"Yes. I've purified the wound..." Ebrill was stammering.

Ksenia looked around her slowly. "Where's Slavka? I owe her a slap," she grunted.

"In the temple, on top of a statue of the largest bird I've ever seen," Evander panted. "She mentioned relics. I think we might be on to something, Ebrill."

"It's not a bird," Ksenia muttered, bringing her head up with some effort.

"What?" Evander looked to her. "Do please stay down, that was a Chasm of a gut punch you took."

"It's a big, winged reptile," Ksenia continued. "And don't you tell me what to do, Maytoni. Lift me up." It was a voice Ksenia had not used since her days as Quartermaster aboard the Daemon Flamingo – she liked the sound of it.

"The wound's sealed. I've dulled the pain too," Ebrill was explaining. "But pirate commander or no, pastorals outrank anybody." She smirked, sassily.

"My bow and quiver!" Ksenia called out, and Alejandro passed the items to her.

Lumbering on sea-legs, Ksenia hauled herself up the steps. The Lady of Feathers clattered through the portal, into the rounded chamber with its crumbling pillars. In the centre stood – as she suspected – a statue of a greater spearhead.

Upon the left wing Slavka stood, one hand gripping the neck for balance. In her other was the small crossbow. From a sculpted bird-of-prey beak sprang another bolt. Spiralling from it came arcs of energy, consuming the surrounding light.

Ksenia was plunged into darkness temporarily. Once the bolt struck tiled floor, the light was released again. Ksenia didn't hesitate, and loosed her arrow at the figure, thumb coming of the string frantically, plucking the projectile to the right.

Another bolt sprang, and darkness arced out in jagged whips. As the abyss was about to engulf her once more, an amber blaze slammed into the darkness. The tendrils of shadow reeled, and the bolt exploded in mid-flight. Behind Ksenia, Alejandro stood, his phoenix arrows in hand.

Evander was like a blur as he whipped by, skidded down to one knee, and drew on Slavka, loosing his arrow and striking her left shoulder.

Slavka leapt from the statue, growling, and ripped out the arrow. The wound glowed with golden energy and sealed. As Evander and

Ksenia nocked new arrows, Slavka backheeled the base of the statue, the weakened rubble giving way.

From the whirls of dust, Slavka pulled a cloth wrapped item and clutched it to her chest. From the length of the material, Ksenia knew that it had to be a bow.

Ebrill's eyes blazed, however Evander's remained hard and focused. Alejandro fixed the arrows back into his bow's quiver, covering the heat.

"This is what I came for," Slavka seethed. "Your so-called god's bow... Which one wielded this?"

Stepping forward, Ebrill spoke calmly, "You tell us. Evey and I are only here to see this statue."

Slavka hesitated before speaking. "I'm ahead of you, then. Your church will pay a king's ransom for this."

One arm clutched the shrouded bow, whilst the other held the crossbow, aimed directly at Ebrill. Ksenia was beginning to wonder just how sharp a shot the summiteers were; Evander was still, his thumb about the string, ready to draw.

"Which one was Senphire?" Slavka pressed herself back into the base of the statue, the sculpted creature looming over her, dwarfing everyone present.

"She beautified the world," Ebrill replied, as if answering a casual inquiry. "At the start, nature was so dark and hostile to us that Senphire loosed an arrow from her bow which restrained the land, sea, and sky. But that bow, Slavka, it absorbed all that hostility. So much fierceness resides in it that it's useless to any mortal." Ebrill began to laugh. "The church won't want it! There's no one the world over who could hold it, unbound by that cloth, never mind use it. It is, by the dangers it has absorbed, harmless. Because not a person exists who could endure that level of unrestrained wildness."

"The Gods love irony," Ksenia blurted out.

"Put it down," Evander said. "Walk away. We're done. Disappear somewhere and be someone else's problem."

Ksenia could have sworn the featureless eyes of Slavka's mask narrowed at him.

Slavka shook her head. "Not a chance. Even *if* any of that's true, you have no idea what I have had to do, to build up the most vicious company the world over, and to come back from your betrayal!"

"Nobody was betrayed," Evander snarled. "*We* acted! When you have a soul, it yearns for what's right. It rebels at the thought of non-action when people are in need!"

"Unravel it if you think I'm wrong," Ebrill said calmly.

Behind the group came the rumble of a volcano. The lion stalked its way into the temple, an expression of bitterness over the regal face. *Not again*, Ksenia thought. She whirled about and said a prayer to the God of Wings and Talons for forgiveness.

Before the beast could leap at anyone, Ebrill had an arm out and the lion halted. Ebrill stared into the amber eyes, and the beast saw something, something Ksenia didn't. It gave a whine and left.

"Did I just witness something...?" Ksenia whispered, looking to Alejandro for explanation. He was as lost as her.

This lull however gave Slavka the opening she wanted. She sent a bolt at Alejandro. Ksenia and Evander loosed arrows a fraction of a second after. Ebrill yelped. Both arrows pierced into Slavka, high in her torso, and she collapsed, dropping Senphire's bow. With a shimmer of golden light, Slavka faded away and was gone, much to Ksenia's confusion.

"What!?" She panted.

Evander gave a guttural sigh before turning to look at Ksenia. "She's escaped. Magical defences. In the event of a loss of consciousness, she can teleport elsewhere. Damn it to the Chasm."

"We hit her in the chest, with two arrows. She's not coming back from that," Ksenia said, though as she spoke couldn't believe her own words. "Right?"

"Don't worry about it," was all Evander said, before he moved to check the others.

From his side, Alejandro pulled out the bolt – without even a grunt. Ebrill rose. She dusted herself down and instantly began looking for his wound.

"Oh, don't worry," he began. "The leviathan leather kills the momentum, and I use an old Hasjin trick, wearing an underlayer of silk; the bolt may penetrate the leather, but it won't penetrate the silk and I can remove it without further injury." He held his side, rubbing it in mild discomfort.

"Silk! In this heat!" Ksenia blurted out, both angry and relieved. "How are you standing!?"

"Well, I get the impression you've walked away from worse," Evander jested, watching him curiously.

"The wound is superficial. Let's see to this bow and statue." Alejandro waved them off.

Ksenia looked down to her own wound. She had known wounds before and fought through them like they weren't there. But in the still and quiet, the wound truly was gone. "That's some magic, Ebrill. Thank you. You must have a _Chasm_ of a will."

"Oh, no. That's the difference between the pastorals and magical practitioners. I don't do anything. Rather, the power of the Gods works through me," Ebrill explained. "I don't have the knowledge, or training for magic. From healing your wound, to taming that lion... None of that was truly me."

Alejandro stalled as he heard the words. "No magically training at all? Nothing?"

"Not a thing. We're forbidden from learning magic, to prevent 'false' miracles."

"Now that's something," Alejandro chuckled to himself. "Maybe there is something to your beliefs."

With some kind of normality restored, Ksenia could finally take in the sight. Whilst this was a stone carving, the singular type of ferocity radiating from its majesty was no less powerful than if they were seeing one in the wild.

The leathery wings extended vastly, coming from a disproportionately tiny body. Yet, the oddest feature was the colossal head at the end of a thin elongated neck, making Ksenia wonder how it could keep its head up at all. And the beak, two thirds of the head, could swallow her whole.

Running down the neck to the shoulders, were sculpted in fine detail, feathers, like a mantle.

"What is it?" Evander said in awe. "We've got nothing like it in The Sigel."

Alejandro answered, "Over here, they're known as, well, it translates to, the eclipse. You can see why. Dragons and such are one thing but look at this beast. I saw a few, a long time ago, out west."

"Ebrill, you know colour. Take a look at the feathers. I'll secure the bow," Evander began then turned to Ksenia. "With your permission, Ksenia."

"What, if I say no, you're not going to take it?" Ksenia said flatly.

"We're not looters. But you or Alejandro should hang on to it."

"I thought no one could use it, that it's too powerful?"

"Some of that was true," Ebrill shouted from behind the statue. "But... some of it was a bluff. And if anyone *could* hold *that* bow and endure its power, it'd be Slavka."

The painter in Ebrill had discerned the colours of the winged beast to be a matching shade for the flights, which had both her and Evander very excited.

Senphire's bow was a boon, and Ksenia decided to let Evander, or rather, the Maytoni have it. Bravenasil's government would only leave it exposed to thieves or sell it on the sly.

Last came the issue of the phoenix arrows.

At Alejandro's cottage, they sat outside in the cool, drinking more wine - something from the cellar. Everyone was too tried to argue, and by this stage, Ksenia could see the bonds between them, and how Evander looked to Alejandro, holding him in high regard.

"If Aeker can vouch for you, I suppose Maytoni can trust you. Besides, having went up against something like Slavka, with the restraint you showed, not immolating the place, we won't bother you – but we're still going to keep an unintrusive eye on you," Evander explained.

"After annihilating a Dytrentian legion, I'd describe me as restrained too," Alejandro said drolly.

Evander waved a hand. "Dytrentians don't count."

"It's all academic," Alejandro added, placing his wine down, a half-smirk breaking over his face. "You can take the arrows, but I can always make more. I never _found_ them. I found the feathers, the correct wood, and the magical know-how to make them."

A surprised silence followed, and then Ksenia spoke. "Not even _I_ knew that."

Part IV – The Dominator Bear

It was blood alright; Luciana Doran knew. Animal blood was one thing, but this was human, and that was going to be a hassle to get out.

"Devastation, that belongs to dragons," she began. "But this... this is obliteration..."

It had been a village, with every building hewn from timber and organised into a logical infrastructure; a street of traders leading into a main square, with residences behind it; all smouldering, the remnants of businesses, hissing in the rain with faint, angry embers here and there. The mayoral residence stood. However, where the wide, welcoming door should have been, a tremendous wound glared. Debris and refuge, splinters, and panels of what had been a barricade lay scattered throughout the pools of blood – *no*, Luci thought, *a damned lake of blood*.

Disconcertingly, the residence had been built for a siege. It was the only building with stone walls behind the wood. Not a castle, but something for the residents to flee into in the event of brigands.

"Here," the tough voice of Tegfan Fielder called out, taking Luci's and Orion's attention.

Their guide, Commander Fielder was six-two, with short dull brown hair and course stubble over a rough, well creased face.

He rose and moved away so they could see what he had been looking at, boots squelching in the sucking mud.

"Fourteen inches by eleven..." Orion muttered with glee, crouched next to the animal print. His eyes went to the runnels above the impact point. He drew a flint knife, and gingerly placed the blade into the tears in the dirt to gauge the depth. The tip came back clean each time.

He turned and smirked at Luci. "You've killed every recorded bear known, isn't that right, Luciana!" He called out, loud enough for Tegfan and the other soldiers looking about the wreckage to hear. Then he broke into a roar, a challenge, "Every known species, but one!"

Luci couldn't help but break into a grin as she stood over this impact crater of a bear paw print, her broken, shimmering reflection sneering back, through the ripples caused by the rain.

Onyx Den was the hunting lodge to end all hunting lodges.

It was small, only housing around two hundred. Ugly pikes embedded in slanted walls reaching fifty feet surrounded the hill, built from the hardest, most enduring rock known, and reinforced with steel. A spire reached up and out of the centre of the mound, like a colossal pike looking to pierce the sky. Sculpted into the walls, facing outward, were images of rooks, with their scythe-like beaks – some open in frozen cries, others pointed upwards to the sky with dignified poise. Giant crossbow emplacements were installed every twenty metres, with braziers imbuing a forlorn glow to the grim atmosphere that hung perpetually over the fortress. Within the mound were the training facilities and personal quarters.

"We told them... Told them, told them, told them – when one attacks, scatter, make for the nearest outpost," Tegfan collapsed into his highbacked chair, deflated. "Instead, they piled into the *one* building, where they were trapped. What was the final count?"

"Thirty-seven dead, five unaccounted for," a hunter replied flatly, as if used to delivering such news.

Whilst in the capital, Orion had received a message from an old friend, Tegfan Fielder, a message with terrible yet exhilarating news. Commander Fielder of the Scared Foresters held a singular role within Bravenasil; to the south of the country was a temperate climate, with petrified forests and steely mountains, home to one of Anordaithe's most dangerous animals, so exceptionally brutal that a whole army force was dedicated to patrolling this southern region to keep watch for them – the dominator bear.

Whilst sightings and encounters were rare, one would find a tucked-away village, then the maneater became an unstoppable killer.

Luci sat in a hard chair, shifting constantly, cursing herself for becoming too accustomed to the luxury of the Castle. Orion sat, a casual air about him as he leaned on Tegfan's oak desk, tankard in hand. Like most of the land in this region, Tegfan's quarters where stuffy and gloomy. A few hunting tapestries hung on the walls, with shelves holding tomes and a mangled bow, a four-foot spear head bent at a neat right angle, and an armoured helm crumbled inwards on all sides.

Tegfan nodded for the scout to leave, no doubt feeling decades older than he was. Hunting was supposed to be exhilarating. Tribulations were a part of it, Luci knew, and if they weren't, it wasn't being done right, but the goal was to feel elated.

"Wouldn't be so bad if people listened."

"Ha!" Luci barked. "You can't help people who won't listen."

"You've done all you can," Ori added. "Still, Luci and I are here." He cast a knowing nod to her, and Luci smirked darkly.

Tegfan looked thoughtful, and old, though Luci knew he was only fifty – eight years younger than Ori, and only three years older than her. "It's been two years since one came our way, and even then," he paused, eyes sinking away into a fogginess. "The tally was thirty-two civilians, and fifteen of our own. Gods, my poor wife," he cackled wickedly, "Though maybe she's given up on me completely. I can't recall the last time getting into an argument about my work. Anyway, I'm out at the end of the year. My daughters are building a farm, and I plan to work it with them."

Tegfan Fielder had known Ori almost seventeen years. Whilst he had never made a formal application to the Castle, Orion, upon being voted in Chair, granted Tegfan membership for his services in this specific field. It broke Luci's heart that Tefgan's experience of hunting had been so dire, and the news of retirement perked her up.

"About time, old man," Ori jested. "I'll send my galleon over, put you and the family up in the

Castle. Your wife and daughters will love Wetsven, and us three can go off hunting."

"Two weddings to pay for, did I mention that?" Tegfan chuckled through his throaty voice. "I can't have them running about somewhere as opulent as Wetsven."

"Have 'em aboard my galleon," Ori said. "I'm serious. We can deck it out however your daughters want, and it can hold an army."

"And if you don't fancy their betrothed, I'm sure they can stumble overboard..." Luci added, grinning.

"Well, first I need to make it out of this mess." Tegfan rose, his white longbow used as a prop to help him up.

"We're slaying this beast, chief," Luci said, certain of it – more certain than anything she had ever said before.

Many of the hunters were in awe of Orion Aldenberg, sharing stories about him, from the legend of him slaying a behemoth to how he managed to take a hydra – setting in place the standardised hunting methods now used.

"He had these crescent shaped arrowheads," one hunter was whispering, as Luci stood with her back to them, pretending she couldn't hear. "The Chanjion ones, used to dismember..."

"What? Really?" Another hunter added.

"What Orion did with the hydra was genius; because whichever head is the right one, the one which won't split into *two* more, is different on every animal, he shot these arrows under the jaw, where the armoured skin ends. The arrow penetrates the flesh, and with force alone breaks the bone of the neck. But the momentum of the arrow is dead, stuck in the neck without going the whole way through, leaving the head still attached..."

There was silence for a moment.

"So, the head is decapitated, sort of – limp, but dead. And can't split."

Luci stood in a vast training hall, imbued with warm white light, and a chimney built into the centre. A wide archery range stretched down one half of the cave for a hundred yards, with archers poised along a designated line, loosing arrows at numerous targets, from round paper faces to large models of bears. What was unusual however, was their equipment. Whilst Orion and Tegfan favoured longbows, and she preferred a hornbow, these soldiers were equipped with a mechanical oddity: a short riser held short limbs, arcing back sharply. Instead of limb tips for a string, small cams held the string in a compact pully system.

She had heard of such bows. When the string was pulled back, the pully system took a large portion of the draw weight away from the archer, and better still, the archer could hold the bow at full draw, almost indefinitely, without any of its strength falling away.

They were ugly to look at, but from a practical standpoint, a life saver. That second it took to draw was a second too late hunting a dominator. With these bows, the archer could move at full draw.

On the other half of the cave, close quarters training took place, with soldiers sparring, wielding either tall halberds or long hunting daggers, ridged with nasty serrations.

Across the walls were shelves of equipment, sconces, and trophies. With hunting came success, or failure. In this line of work, it was victory or defeat. It was odd, Luci thought, looking at the slaying of an animal from a military perspective. This wasn't hunting at all, it was war.

Like glaring warnings, gigantic skulls of this bear had been placed on pillars throughout the cave; wide, long snouts with malicious fangs.

One trophy stood above all others, however. A full sized, taxidermized beast, nine feet tall standing up on two legs, and glaring down at her, and everyone else it seemed, with all the unrelenting judgment that would come from a god.

In a way, it was her God. Luci had slain all known species of bear, some larger than a dominator, but none held the same level of reverence as it. These were the animals which made her who she was, that gave her live beyond the dregs of existence; from the feral arena girl to the world-renowned huntress, she was now.

Luci never knew her parents, if she had been abducted or sold, but she began life in servitude, forced to fight animals for entertainment. From an early age she learned to hate bears.

Then eighteen years ago, Orion appeared. Disgusted at what he saw, he turned his bow and hunting posse on the syndicate running the fights and pulled her from that feral world into a life more human.

For all the civilisation instilled into her, though, Luci still hated bears on a deeply, primal level. It was a feud, manufactured by nature, transcending personal grudges or revenge; this was when one apex predator exists at the same time as another.

Both eyes were spread wide, and forward facing, like many of its species, thus ensuring tremendous eyesight. The nose, a thick, leather stub, held the ability to smell just about anything from miles away – and pick out the scent of human sweat and blood above everything else. The claws were longer than any Luci had seen on a bear, glinting like scimitars, with many serrations and potential to eviscerate and dismember prey.

"They can move faster than a chariot," a women said from behind. Pulled from the reverie, Luci turned to see a hunter, as tall as her, but younger by nearly a decade. "Siani Binsaighter." She extended the most gnarled, scared hand, Luci had ever seen. The skin was all ravaged scar tissue. She took the hand nonetheless and introduced herself.

"Luci, they call me."

"I know, who you are. I was surprised to hear that you've never slain a dominator," Siani went on, looking the trophy up and down with something close to reverence too. The woman was all angular, hard features with a shaved head, dark stubble coming through but intersected by a whip-strike scar over her crown. "I'll be there with you, no doubt, when the boss sends us out. Three quarters of the hunting teams are veterans, have to be, otherwise we'd get slaughtered. And at least two must have slain a beast in the past."

"You've slain one of those," Luci couldn't help but sound envious. "Magnificent."

"Always comes at a cost... And a body count." Siani held her hand up again. "They call it 'getting gloved'. The beast had my arm in its maw, and as I tried to pull it out, it bit down, taking the skin off... Of course, I hardly noticed, what with the blood pouring from the gouge in my skull." Her tone was so matter of fact it was almost unsettling. Luci wondered what scars she would bare after this clash, to tell the world of her apotheosis – she looked forward to them.

"Mage work?" Luci ventured.

"Yeah, but I can't afford any extra work to get the scars removed."

"Why would you? Scars tell the best stories, and that is better than any medal they could give you, surely?"

Siani looked reflective, but only nodded. She looked to the command table beyond Luci, to where Orion and Tegfan leaned over maps with a few other soldiers standing by. The table itself was built out of the ribcage of a dominator, yellowing pikes running along the edges, with the main support coming from skeletal legs and arms, all holding up a slate of rock.

"Whilst many hunters utilise as much of the animal as possible, we use all the parts of a dominator we can for display, to remind people that they can, in fact, be killed," Siani explained, answering Luci's unspoken query.

The pair approached the table, where Tegfan was looking older then he had before.

"The nearest town is there," one soldier, with enchanted prosthetics replacing both arms and legs, pointed out. "I've got scouts waiting there with local militia, just in case, but the beast hasn't made an appearance."

Siani leaned into Luci and whispered, "That's Acer Santiago. Been with us eight years, and yes, both legs and arms are artificial – had them ripped off by a beast three years ago. Should have died." Dismemberment was a standard attack for most bears, to prevent its prey from fleeing whilst it tucked in, Luci knew.

"Acer must have the blood of demigods to come back from that," Luci muttered. He was the tallest of the group, with dark blonde hair and bright brown eyes, and contrasting black facial hair like soot over his lower face.

"Most likely it's next target," Tefgan muttered. He looked to Ori. "Of course, it's unlikely to go there now, after filling its belly. We need to get to it before it grows hungry again."

"What have your scouts found in terms of a trail?" Ori asked, looking the calmest around the grim table.

"Bits and pieces," Acer answered. "Odds and ends for the ones in the hospitallers to match up."

If these were the survivors, what was the average life expectancy of one of these soldiers? Luci wondered.

"The marrow rooks are betraying the beast, as usual," Acer continued. "Flocks of them have been sighted across Havicore Gorge, picking at the leftovers."

"Marrow rooks often follow the dominators," Siani explained. "They scavenge on the marrow in the bones of the dead, hence the name. In our history, rooks have never been associated with anything positive, and when a large flock is sighted, it either precedes, or follows a dominator attack."

"Typical, one way in and one way out... Plenty of foliage, sheer mountain faces on either side, and river too. Can strike and then withdraw and disappear," Tegfan mused, drumming fingers over the dense stone. His face conveyed the thought no one was saying aloud, as if it would be bad luck, but they all knew, even Luci, that this was going to be a challenge.

Scouts led by Acer moved through the petrified forest. Their mechanical bows had arrows nocked as they moved over the isolated terrain. Their attire was thick and luxurious and would have been the envy of many a citizen elsewhere on the continent. Around their collars, cuffs, and boots, tufts of dark-gold fur trimmed their leather tunics and breeches. Over this lay scaled, bronze armour. Some scouts had talons and fangs adorning their outfits, functioning as clasps and others had bunches of rook feathers tied up over their breast or upper arms for luck.

Against the dank atmosphere of dead trees, they looked like predators themselves. Even their faces, from the greenest solider to the most senior, were twisted into a single-minded awareness from which no leaf rustle or change in the direction of the breeze would be missed.

For once, Luci felt like the unbloodied hunter.

Their path was up a slope, twisting, gnarled trees reaching up, as if crying out for light. A mile either side of the group held rocky surfaces breaking out from the muddy ground, with a myriad of flowing rivers breaking through the debris of shattered trunks, branches, and stone. The whole gorge resembled the aftermath of a cyclone. Then, to frame their tunnel into this beast's den, the huge mountains on either side conspired to keep the sun from shining down into the gorge, as the group moved north to south, keeping them in perpetual dusk.

"Smell that," one scout said, looking to Siani.

"Yeah, that's death," she sighed. Luci could only catch the mould in the air and the sharp tang of water.

Siani's attire was slightly different to the others, in that her toe-points held curved bear claws which could eviscerate with ease. Along her arms and thighs were many fangs, all arranged by size and reinforced with steel underneath. This was to prevent the bear from trying to dismember her, should one get that close. Over her chest were the shattered fragments of a dominator's colossal skull, mapped out for display as well as protection – a fitting parallel to the scar running over her own crown.

"You're the death god of bears," Luci had whispered to her before leaving. "Their death deity manifested."

In comparison, Luci wore a composite steel-bone armour, extremely light weight as magical properties of the behemoth bone absorbed the weight of the steel, all the while providing exceptional protection, with grey and blonde fur around the collar, trimming the belt and straps, and claws and fangs utilised for clasps.

Ori and Tegfan were leading a flanking force off to the right, with pikes and longswords, ready to blindside the beast. Before leaving, Ori had given Luci something remarkably special, even by the standards of the crazy world they lived in. It was known by some as the Crowned Bow, by others as the Vainglory Bow. This mythical item had been found in the guts of the behemoth Orion slew, and until then, no one ever assumed it was real. The entire bow was jet, fossilised wood, and was about the densest thing Luci had ever held. Yet, it functioned as a bow should. The twist was that the bow had been crafted with magic, ensuring it could only ever be drawn on a target whose slaying was deemed 'worthy' by nature; the string and limbs would not yield otherwise. Ori had decided that a dominator bear met the criteria, and Luci hoped he was correct. Aside from the bow, she had twin blades fixed to her hips, small, wide daggers with horizontal grips, designed for sudden close quarters fighting.

As the valley narrowed, tightening into a rocky rise, Siani drew her mechanical bow. Luci jolted with excitement; however, the hunter was only 'glassing' the area. A magical interface shimmered into place beside the riser, through which the world became a blur of brighter colours as the growing dark was filtered out.

"I don't like this ground..." One scout said, tapping soft moss with a boot. "Doesn't-"

Whatever notion he had, was lost as nature's fury erupted upwards in a tornado of rock, dirt, and human gristle. Luci spun to see the bloody remains of the hunter splatter to the ground before their foundation collapsed.

The path had been an old river basin, they discovered too late, detritus piled up and rotted down over centuries. Amongst the dank rot, Luci found her bearings fast, senses sharpening automatically. Around her, the mounds of accumulated compost tumbled to create a clearing. Another scream, and Luci saw a scout slashed, head to groin by bloody talons. For a moment the collapsing strips of the body where all she saw, then the giant came into focus; on its hind legs, burnt golden fur with rich brown tips. It was at least ten feet tall. Its scent was constricting, humid and meaty, and threatened to choke Luci.

But she was far from overwhelmed. Luci raised the bow, an arrow already on the string, its broadhead fashioned from bear fang and claw. The bear roared, and Luci roared back, loosing the arrow. However, the beast dropped to all fours and charged, the arrow striking the tall lump of its shoulders and bouncing away.

More arrows from hunters whipped into its flanks, with Siani to the left, caked in mire. The beast's charge was stalled as it was overwhelmed by the sudden numbers. This lasted for half a second and as one scout tried to take advantage of its daze, the bear turned and swallowed her head whole in its maw. The hunter's shriek was struck down by the crumpling of the helmet. The bear then tore the head from the shoulders in a spray of blood. With a wet and gut-wrenching crunch, the head was swallowed whole.

Ori and the flanking guard tore in, roaring like wild animals. Halberds with huge blades, too large to take up against any human, swept across the dank field. The bear swatted several aside, but one made contact, only for its point to shear and snap. The bear brought a paw down shattering the shaft. It then fell on the hunter, front paws flattening the torso of the large man completely, severing the arms and head.

In the flurry of madness, Luci managed to get a point of aim at the lungs and loosed the arrow. But the bear swivelled, sensing the change in wind from the shot. Dark eyes locked on her. It charged again.

Luci dropped the bow and grabbed her blades. The beast loomed over her, swallowing the world entirely. Roaring, she charged, as it came down over her, Luci dropped to a slide thrusting wildly at its gut before careening out from between its stubbier legs. The satisfying warmth of blood graced her hands, but the joy was short lived as the beast swung around, a paw raking her back. Shrieking steel pierced Luci's ears as her armour tore open, the behemoth bone taking the brunt of the hit, but failing against the bear's might.

Instead of trepidation, Luci felt elated. Something that could crush behemoth bone! There was no greater bear in all the world for her and this was the summit of her struggles and trials. She whipped around throwing a dagger into the bears maw as it tried to snap at her head. Fangs tore through her gauntlets, and she couldn't tell which blood belonged to her, or to the bear. With her other hand she drove the second blade into the neck. Thick hide fought the blade, and Luci didn't have the time to thrust again. She pulled her arms back as it recoiled, then a paw swung toward her. There was the sky, the blurs of the environment, and Luci was on her side, struggling to breath. Her whole breastplate had been sheered into shrapnel. She tensed her chest, holding her breath, rather than struggle to breath. Blood trickled down from her mouth, down the side of her head and from her broken nose.

The flanking guard had almost surrounded the beast, however, its back swings ripped chests open and obliterated faces, dropping hunters. Luci turned and scrambled for the bow. Taking hold of it, she rose and nocked an arrow. When the beast rose on its hind legs, a hunter held in its drooling maw, she sent an arrow into its gut. A guttural roar greeted the hit. It shook the man away. Luci loosed another arrow into its gut and the bear crumbled back to all fours. It was not wincing but readying for a charge. Luci was in the process nocking another arrow before she realised this, and the beast launched itself like a boulder from a trebuchet; the speed should have been beyond its size. Luci rolled to the right. When the gigantic paws hit the muck, the whole edge of the dank bank collapsed, and Luci found herself caught in the collapse, swallowed by muck, filth, dead wood, and water.

What passed for light came over her eyes as she slid, backwards down a rocky bank. Her whole body was mired in stagnant muck, twigs, and dead leaves as if she had just crawled out of her own grave. She spat out a mouthful of detritus, burning with eagerness for another shot. Luci still had the bow in hand, and no force in the natural world was going to shake it from her.

On her back, looking up the bank, Luci nocked another arrow. The dominator was only ten yards off, a colossal monument to nature's fury, on its hind legs. Muck and mire were smeared over its legs, bloody drool falling in torrents from its slavering maw, and flesh and gristle hung from its upper paws. Its fur and hide were so thick that the bloody wounds Luci and the hunters had inflicted upon it were not visible.

This animal stood like an immortal beast, nature personified, just as Ori had said. No matter how much harm they can inflict on nature, there will always be something else, something new to push back against them.

Leaning up, too cold to feel any pain from the numerous injuries she had, Luci drew the bow as best she could in such a position and loosed.

The arrow sprang and caught the bear's jaw, it cried out balefully as a paw covered its mouth. Luci had another arrow nocked and sent it into a knee joint. The beast's leg quivered, and it brought the other forward to compensate for the sudden unbalance. However, the mire was far from solid footing, and caved in, toppling the beast.

The landslide of fur and anger crashed over Luci, and all went black.

Suffocation brought Luci back into consciousness. She pulled her face from icy waters and drew in breath with a howl. Nerves tumbled through her body, like lumpen shot, as the memory of the dominator came back to her.

Rising, Luci found the bow under her. She brought her head up, her whole face throbbing and had it not been devoid of feeling, she was sure the agony would put her back into unconsciousness. Her nose was going to need major mage work – if it was still there.

Then the clamp came over right her arm and she was wrenched back. Shrieking in animalistic fury rather than pain, Luci heard the crack, followed by the heat of her own blood spurting over her face. Growling, using the heat of the blood to reinvigorate her, Luci rolled onto her front, grasping for her blades; unaware she was also doing so with the stub of her upper right arm, and plunged the weapon into the bear's guts again. The beast snarled and bounded away. Luci rose, showing indifference to the fact that her right arm had been bitten off, and was now held in the maw of the dominator. Its eyes, full of swirling, unrelenting power, were on her. It clamped both paws over the lower arm and crunched down on the appendage, snapping it up and swallowing the pieces, all the while glaring at Luci.

A part of her had been taken by this beast, and Luci was more determined than ever to take its life. With the bow in her left hand, she managed to fish an arrow from her thigh quiver. Dragon's blood on the shafts would have kept them from getting damaged in the fall. Leaning the arrow against her thigh, Luci gingerly pressed the string of the bow over its grove until it clicked into place and brought the bow up, only now actually realising she was going to have difficulty drawing it.

The beast had to know it had her, Luci thought. It was wary, and damn right too, Luci continued thinking, glowering back as it panted eagerly some fifteen yards away. She clamped her teeth over the nock of the arrow and pushed her left arm out, drawing the bow, but drawing it at a steep cant. Her front teeth ached and felt as if they were about to be launched from her mouth.

The bear roared, and Luci loosed the arrow, sending it down the beast's gullet, the reverse barbs of the pile shredding its throat as the arrow rammed into it. Flailing, blood fountaining from its mouth, the bear fell to its side, coughing, gurgling, and trying its best to roar as it choked on its own blood. Eyes bulging, tongue lolling its claws made one last feeble gesture, pawing at the dirt, and splashing the water before the beast finally went still.

A weak smirk of triumph made its way across Luci's pale lips. Walking on legs with the density of rubber, Luci clambered over to the body. With her only hand, Luci pulled her dagger out, and stabbed at the Dominators jaw, dislodging a fang. Dropping the knife from shaking, weak fingers, she picked up the fang, and used it to add the tally on the Crowned Bow. Three vertical lines had been scratched into the upper part of the riser, by a previous owner or owners, and Luci added a forth... Then, collapsed.

Part V – The Blind Spiders

Brencis Fong was an ambitious man, Ksenia had to give him that. But he was an idiot.

This twat was a member of the Flint Castle. However, instead of finding out about his presence through underground sources, Brencis actually contacted Ksenia himself... Or at least through a messenger, who had shown up at the Kiamount Sanctuary looking for Ksenia, but instead found her younger sister in charge.

There was 'vital information', they needed to hear, to save lives. And Ksenia decided that this was clearly a trap, by a man who was not nearly as clever as he thought. It was too tacky to be from Orion's mind.

The pair had responded to Brencis' message, knowing that if there was a trap, they could side-step it and capture this high-ranking member. Brencis was the treasurer of the Flint Castle, after all. A bold game was being played, Ksenia mused, if three major figures had come to The Mane, all in search of Alejandro.

As it turned out, there was a trap. Not one sprung by Brencis' ingenuity, but by a vicious network of spiders... And Brencis' stupidity. If

Brencis had any value, she and Alejandro were going to have to rescue him before this den of spiders made a beverage of him. These beasts were unhesitatingly responsive, precision strikers – which was something indeed, considering they were blind.

"Dumb, stupid, idiotic, imbecilic..." Ksenia began.

"And many other synonyms," Alejandro finished.

They stood by the entrance to the spider's den, a bank of sheer porous rock with a gaping entry, as if kicked into the cliffside by a giant. From the gash poured acrid scents. It was a sinking whirlpool, sucking in all vainglory, and it sat like a gangrenous sore amongst the hues of greens from the surrounding trees, bejewelled with dew, and ordained in golden rays passing through the foliage, over which a vivid sky shone.

"I'm having second thoughts, which means you're definitely having second thoughts," Ksenia added, glaring into the den.

"Of course, I am. But we've come all this way..." Alejandro sighed and placed his exotic bow back into his leather hip-quiver.

"If anything, we can get proof of death."

"Nothing like a shot of morbidity to fire up one's incentive."

Within the cave opening, the heat died to the shade, and inkiness filled Ksenia's periphery. The walls glistened with ethereal-like minerals, reflecting all manner of sharp, steely greys over countless groves and runnels.

"Here, put this on." Alejandro handed Ksenia a dense, dark purple, leviathan leather face-wrap. "Their webs are so sensitive to sound that they'll even catch you breathing."

Watching the nest of her hair, Ksenia gently pulled the hard leather over her face. Just typical, she mused. "I've never encountered these things before, are you sure?" She said, the rough leather rubbing the tip of her nose with each syllable spoken. This was going to be a bother, alright.

"*Very*," Alejandro whispered, moving ahead with the gentlest and most deliberate of steps. "Heal to toe when walking. Imagine you're barefoot on glass."

As Ksenia imitated Alejandro's sluggish, under-water-like movement, the systems of webs crept into view, covering the ceiling and upper walls of the tunnel. Despite the tunnel's apex at fifteen feet, and the width increasing as they went, the sight of these glistening, bejewelled webs began to make the cavern feel very cramped.

Thick, porcelain white struts and sheets loomed over them, studded with what looked like sapphires and emeralds. A trap of course to lure prey into touching the web, signalling the denizens of their presence and position. Instinctively, Ksenia tucked her hands under her armpits, stroking the smooth barbs of her feathered garment with her thumbs for reassurance.

Prior to arriving, Alejandro had stressed that once they encountered the webs, they would not be able to audibly communicate; the strands so sensitive to any vibration at all, they would pick up on the finest sounds, and alarm the spiders.

Of all the mad and grotesque creatures, why did Brencis have to try hunting these?

Four to five feet across, and five to six feet in length, the giant spiders were blind, designed by nature with no eyes. They preyed on anything disturbing their webs, a sense of touch so acute, they could feel the vibration from a yawn anywhere within their miles' long structures. Then the unfortunate bugger was swarmed by the spiders, their venom ensuring instant paralysis. This, of course, made cocooning an uncomplicated matter, before shifting them off to melt down and slurp up later.

As the light dissolved, a glistening caught Ksenia's eye. She turned to glance at the minerals, squinting close before recoiling, her heart exploding and throwing desperate flight energy throughout her limbs. Only a few feet away, tucked into a hovel, oblivious, was one of the spiders. Despite knowing it was blind, she felt it's eager hunger. Spindly legs stretched out like jagged tentacles, vivid azure blending into darker shades with dull yellow stripes decorating the appendages. Its lean abdomen twinkled as hot white tips of hair contrasted against the waves of blue body colouration. Fangs, curved, translucent, and as thin as large nails, were waiting patiently for her to make a mistake.

When birds had a 'nest', it sounded cute, cosy, but when the word was applied to spiders, it became sinister, making Ksenia's skin crawl.

This nest was hideously large, encompassing a vast cavern with the infestation of web. Structures which looked as dense as rock, bulged from the ceiling, with thinner sheets stretching between them. Stalagmites, countless in number, made movement nearly impossible, with hardly a solid footing available. Upon most, the whirling streams of web met, to give the spiders a path back to specific points in the cave.

All the while, the colours of sapphire and emerald gleamed in what little light remained.

There were no signs of the spiders, however, Ksenia knew full well that they were there, and likely far closer to her than she could guess. There were no signs of bodies, or that any poor bugger had been dragged down here – then again, there would be nothing left by the time the spiders were done with someone. There had better be something left behind of Brencis, she seethed, not sure who or what she was angry at; Brencis for being such a reckless twat, the spiders for making breathing a gruelling affair, or herself for going through with this.

Footing was getting worse, as Ksenia had to place one boot almost, directly in front of the other, like tightrope walking, to get between the stalagmites. As she moved across the lumpen ground, she became self-conscious about her breathing. Shallow breaths were beginning to strain her chest, hardly able to get a deep breath out, to clear her lungs.

Alejandro stopped at a slightly more open space and Ksenia moved in beside him. She caught what had halted him; tucked into a crevasse, a few feet off the ground, was the unmistakable outline of a body, wrapped in web.

It would have been a natural reaction for Ksenia to sigh an obscenity, and she had to squeeze her fists tight to manage her temper. This had better be him, she thought.

Every eventuality she and Alejandro could think of was planned for, thoroughly, because neither would be able to audibly communicate due to the extreme sensitivity of the web. With Brencis wrapped up, it would be impossible to cut him out without alerting every single spider in the cave and tunnels. However, Alejandro had brought with him whistling arrows, normally used to spook horses, and throw off riders, by bandits.

Alejandro drew his flint-dagger and nodded to Ksenia. She held whistling arrows in her hip-quiver, and delicately began to draw one with painful slowness.

Alejandro approached the cocoon, unaffected by the grotesqueness of it. He weighed up where to begin cutting, looking over the body to gauge the thickness of the web and make sure not to harm their whole reason for this ridiculous venture. He turned and nodded to Ksenia, letting her know he was going to begin cutting. Ksenia nodded back and nocked the arrow, pressing her thumb and finger against the nock to prevent any noise. She chose the direction to the right, where it was much wider and the arrow would fly for longer, and began to draw, again, painfully slowly to prevent any creaking from the wood or string. At half draw, the arrow swayed away from the bow. Clenching her teeth, heart bursting, Ksenia watched the arrow dangle from the string, barely fixed by the nock. She held her breath, and was sure Alejandro was doing the same. Terrified to move, unable to without dislodging the nock, she gave a frantic glance towards her partner. Alejandro leaned across and picked up the arrow, keeping it on the string and set it back onto her thumb, by the grip.

Ksenia cursed herself, feeling more frustrated that she couldn't release a sigh to pour out any nervous energy. Keeping her thumb up to hold the arrow in place, Ksenia continued drawing. She could see Alejandro in her periphery, waiting for her to reach full draw. Once she was there, the grip on his dagger visibly tightened and he plunged it into the cocoon.

Eagerly, Ksenia loosed the arrow and the cry of a dyeing banshee trilled from the pile. At the same time, she let out a much-needed breath. The cry of the arrow fell away into the darkness of the cave, and instantly, all around her, were excited stirrings. The ceiling web bulged in countless spots as spiders raced in the direction of the sound, or rather followed the vibrations carried through the web. To her right and left, the creatures appeared as if from nowhere, their gangling, knobbly legs moving at blurring speed as they effortlessly covered walls of web between stalagmites and stalactites. One even pulled itself through a bundle of web only a few feet above Ksenia, scuttling around a stalactite and away.

For reasons Ksenia could not fathom, she was suddenly very cold, though every nerve ending in her body was on alert as she tried to ignore just how many of the spiders there where, and just how close she and Alejandro had been to them.

Alejandro had torn a great gash in the cocoon; however, it had not breeched all the way through, and another thick layer had been revealed. He nodded to Ksenia, signalling he was going to try again, and she moved to take another arrow from her quiver. As she gingerly drew the arrow, her fingers slipped from the nock, and it tumbled to the ground with a tinkle of metal against rock. Her heart seized, but she grasped the arrow and nocked it in a flurry of panicked movements. Alejandro braced himself to begin cutting, and Ksenia reached full draw, fast. He hurriedly plunged the dagger into the web and thrust down, and Ksenia loosed in the same direction as before. Fury and agony soared into the far darkness.

Finally, they had a boon, and Ksenia could see the tanned face of a man peeking out from the cocoon, eyes wide in fear. Alejandro was about to pull the man out in one mighty tug, but from nowhere, a spider scuttled in their direction. It then halted over Brencis' cocoon, as if waiting for something. The hunter's eyes widened even more, as if they might burst from their sockets. At least this twat was wise enough to keep quiet. However, the spider scuttled off to join its colony on the other side of the cavern. With a mighty grasp, Alejandro pulled Brencis from the web, bringing sheets and tendrils of the cocoon with him. Ksenia loosed another arrow to cover this action, then Alejandro nodded for her to move.

Escaping the den was still an arduous affair, but Brencis retained the wit to stay quiet, and the trio worked their way out as the spiders collected around the far end of the cave in a frenzy.

Never had the fusion of greens, blues, browns, and golds looked like paradise. Back in the forest, Brencis staggered, trying to pull the clumps of web from his attire, only for the strands to swallow up his hands.

"Thank you..." He began, however, with a channel cleared for her anger, Ksenia walloped her forehead into the man's face. Brencis reeled, eyes fluttering, arms wide and searching for leverage, then collapsed. Ksenia moved in with a raised fist before a cool hand checked her.

"I said you could hit him *once*," Alejandro spoke, wearily.

Composing herself, Ksenia stalked away, pulling the wrap from her face, taking in the purified air. On his back, and scuttling into the roots of a tree, Brencis whimpered.

"Hey, look I said I was going to help you, what was that?" He panted; the words muffled by a hand clutching his nose. He was lean with light bronze skin. His almond eyes were tree-trunk brown, and a coarse goatee framed his mouth for a mature appearance.

"Brencis, you had better have something good for us! I've been around many dangerous animals in my time, but that was excruciating, so we *are* getting something from you," Alejandro seethed. He pulled his face wrap away, revealing the glass-scars.

"What? Can't you speak properly?" Brencis removed his hand from his swollen, purple nose, blood smeared down his mouth and chin.

"Okay, you can hit him again."

Unhesitatingly, Ksenia marched across the soft dirt and threw her boot into the man's groin. Brencis howled and recoiled into a ball, whining, and panting.

"We still need him to talk, though," Alejandro added.

"That's why I didn't kick him in the face," Ksenia retorted. She pulled the hunter to his knees. He clutched both thighs, bracing himself upright, panting heavily, struggling for breath.

"Hey, look, I'm willing to talk," Brencis managed. He looked up into Alejandro's cold eyes and seemed to search the scars on the left side of his face. "I bet you don't know why Orion is after you, eh? I overheard him, talking to Luci about it. *And* I know his plan, to lure you out... Gods, it's bad. He's going too far. Even Luci wouldn't approve if she knew it."

Ksenia froze at the mention of the names, her temper stilled momentarily. Alejandro remained quiet, standing over Brencis like a beacon of judgment.

"I doubt he discussed this *grand plan* with her then," Ksenia broke in. "So how did you get wind of it?"

"Amdt Aakster, our expedition manager. His morals fall more in line with Orion's. With Luci and Orion here, Amdt is running the Castle,"

Brencis replied. "That Dytrentian Prince, the one who tried to get a place in the Castle..."

Alejandro furrowed his brow, thinking for a moment.

"That was a setup, to see if you were real," Brencis continued.

Ksenia looked to Alejandro to try and discern something from his frozen face. Her blood was chilled, though she felt a personal twinge of acid in her heart, that Alejandro had been played like that, that she had in fact been played and fallen so stupidly for it too, having been the one to throw the information out into the ether, knowing it would get to Alejandro.

As if sensing her thoughts, Alejandro gave her a reassuring look, and a subtle hand gesture stayed her next words. Ksenia swallowed, dryly then went back to Brencis. "And you fled here, to warn us? Somehow, I don't think it's that simple."

Brencis wiped blood from his mouth. "I came out here, unbeknownst to the Castle, to see if you were real too."

"And to see if you could take me out," Alejandro finished for him.

Both of Brencis' hands came up, covered in web, soaked dark pink by blood. "No... I mean, yes. There's no way Orion would have let me try my hand at hunting you. You're his. But I thought

I could go after you, and then spin a tale to Orion that you ambushed me whilst I was hunting wildebeest or something... Get the glory, and I don't have to worry about Orion's wrath. But after you took out Baily, the cometeer, I had a change of heart. Being able to out-duel someone like him, well, I thought better of confronting you. I've jumped into enough deep ends in my life to know when one is going to swallow you whole."

Alejandro glanced to the cave, then to Brencis. "Sure."

"Hey, I had to get something out of this trip. And those venom glands could build me a castle or two."

Ksenia sighed. "So, you became worried that we might figure out you're here, and *actually* ambush you whilst hunting."

"Start talking. If I like what I hear, I won't feed you to Ksenia," Alejandro spoke coolly, folding his arms.

"Right, yes! Well, this has nothing to do with revenge. And he doesn't want your arrows – weirdly, he detests them. He won't come for you directly either. Orion knows better. No, he's going to draw you out..."

18 years ago...

Eitimovel was the last city state of Moviel.

The Dytrentian Empire had had little issue sweeping over this defiant republic with no unity between its major cities. One at a time, the siege legions of Dytrentia constricted each walled city and squeezed the life from it, before breeching it, ripping its heart out, and burning the body.

Eitimovel was hardly a fraction of the size of its dead neighbours, with no walls to defend it; its only defensive feature was the steep hill it was built on. Every structure was sculpted from wood, beautifully crafted panels, and arches, all a few stories tall. The population was a three thousand and an undisciplined militia of four hundred were its defenders; most couldn't string a bow, nor had the strength to pull one.

Orion Aldenberg knew the city was going to fall, now open to the eight thousand strong army. He did not fancy being a slave, or his chances against so many. He was a hunter, used to vicious cats, or draigs with steamed breath so coarse it could strip skin. He had considered offering his services as a hunter, or even joining their expeditionary units, though the latter was largely looting as opposed to proper exploration of the natural and unknown world.

No. He would try to escape; wait until the chaos in the streets was as its height and use it as cover. What was the point in senselessly throwing himself into this grinder? Besides, he had always wanted to get out of Moviel, and every time something stopped him; first the game in the mountains, then work as a forester, then his wife, and then when she passed, the quagmire of gloom which keeps a person in stagnancy.

Large towers with bulbous turrets surrounded the city. These were nothing more than watch posts, built to hold a few people at a time. Orion stood on the balcony of one, a thousand yards from the legion, using a looking glass to inspect the soon-to-be raiders.

These were only light infantry, but each soldier was hewn from the experience of centuries of warfare. Purple angular armour was wrapped around torsos, arms, and thighs, forged from who-knew what types of metals, leathers, and silks. Various patters in a deep blood red had been worked into the breastplates, gorgets, pauldrons, vambraces, and shin guards. Every soldier present had a rich yellow cloak hanging from their left shoulder, upon which was the Dytrentian Empire's insignia. Masks covered every face, and these were unique to each army, their defining insignia. In this instance, the masks looked to have been carved from copper, with vines spilling out from the dark eye-sockets and gaping mouths. Orion had no idea what it was supposed to signify, but it was gruesome to look at. Their shields, hexagonal in shape, presented a barrier which looked impossible to break, with glimmers from sabres winking between the ranks.

It was over-kill for Orion's tiny home, and the Dytrentians knew it. This was a show of force, to set an example against resistance. No one was getting out of this alive, or without shackles.

The hills to the cities left could have been utilised at one time or another, with archers, siege equipment, and cavalry, but complacency and a lack of any real order reigned over Eitimovel.

Yet, from those dull green hills, a single figure bounded over the terrain; only a shady mark but moving wildly with purpose. Just what was this person doing? Orion brought the eyeglass around, and caught a man with dark hair, tanned skin, dressed in shabby, beaten leather and linen, and armed with a bow and a quiver of arrows.

Orion chuckled to himself. Then again, maybe there was something noble here; at least someone was standing up to the Dytrentians.

Then again it might have been better to join the Dytrentian Empire. They didn't ask for much, Orion thought, and the benefits were magnificent; they could keep their gods, their government, and culture, in return for taxation, occupation, and recruits. The Dytretians would improve their infrastructure, medicine, farming, and security. Life would be better, and in return all Orion had to do was pretend he cared about some self-appointed Emperor. What was all the fuss about really? People made too much of a controversy with boarders and such. Orion could not have carried less about flags – which is all it came down to in the end – so long as he had the freedom to hunt and explore.

Prior to Moviel's defiance, Orion couldn't see the Dytrentians stopping him from doing either of those. Then again, the Dytrentians were huge purveyors in slave trading, and some of the original Dytrentian states held perverse beliefs regarding superior bloodlines and races. It would be hard to accept the benefits of the empire whilst wading through its murky undercurrents.

From the front ranks of the army, soldier's laughter caught on the breeze; mocking and disbelieving they slackened in their rigidity, waiting to see what this single little man was going to do. Orion was intrigued too.

From the quiver, the man brought out an arrow, the flights glowing orange, like fire. Magic, Orion assumed. Was this fellow a mage? Like it would matter. The Dytrentians would have someone in their ranks to counter anything sent their way. The man snatched his draw hand away from the string, as if something had bitten him, and shook his fingers. Perhaps there was some heat to the flights? He clenched his hand and few times, as if readying himself, the mocking tunes of the soldiers still flowing over the scene. Then, this archer drew the bow, aiming high, and loosed. All the heads of the soldiers in the front ranks followed the arc to its height and watched as it descended, none bothering to raise their shields.

A furious eruption ignited, and the front ranks of the army disappeared into a cauldron of blazing conflagration. All the thunder of nature followed, and Orion felt a wall of force and heat fall over him, even so far away. Rich, bright orange diffused into a soul-wavering darkness. Upon the ground uncountable tendrils of amber ripped through the terrain searching for prey, with talons of inky smoke rising up from the fissures, lunging into the maelstrom of flame and light.

152

Screaming, the despairing cries of those facing inescapable death, caught up to Orion. As the light fell, he saw the ranks of armoured men and women combust or melted down to slag, sought out by the tendrils breaking through the ground, or set upon by the smoky talons. The remaining ranks tried to flee. The archer was struggling back to his knees, his head bowed as if he had just been struck with a mortal wound. Had someone gotten a lucky arrow off in his direction? Couldn't have. Not through that madness. He rose and pulled another arrow from his quiver. Commanders were bawling at their ranks to reorganise and charge as the prestigious presentation of the legion was lost, devolved into a whirlpool of frantic metal.

Another arrow went up, and Orion heard a cry of anguish follow it, with the archer collapsing as if dead. More ranks of soldiers disappeared amongst the fury of another eruption, vaporised as the fire washed through the confusion. Then the tendrils of amber and arcs of smoke ripped into the army once more.

The archer was up again, struggling to straighten, looking like a drunken figure trying to compose himself. He loosed a final time, another of these ferocious arrows into the furnace and finally fell, unmoving.

Just what in all of nature was this!? Tingling trepidation flooded Orion's chest and arms, rippling over his cheeks, whilst awe kept his eyes wide and made him lightheaded. Orion was both amazed and horrified. What power was this? The level of magic in those arrows could never be managed by a single person. All of the anger of nature, its wrath was imbued within the flames rolling over the last of the screaming soldiers, pulsing and flashing in ambers and oranges.

Orion could only think of one thing to which such power belonged and was aghast as to just how this tiny little man, one of his own species had managed to take it and use it. The phoenix was immortal, indestructible, and untameable. It was nature's ultimate expression of its eternity and insuperable state. They were outside the powers of anyone – and according to legend, even demigods.

Just what was this lunatic doing, wielding this power, overstepping into a realm that wasn't for him? This shouldn't be in his possession. Humans could rise to meet nature, that was their purpose, but to rip the crown from Her head and the sceptre from Her hands like this was abominable, it couldn't happen – shouldn't happen. That power was natures and natures alone. No one should be able to hold it, not just because it didn't belong, but the depths of it should have been too much for a mind and body to even manage! Whoever he was, this archer had upset the natural order of the world, and now Orion's whole world, his whole spirt and everything he believed had been run through by this stranger.

Orion decided to climb down from the tower and head across to the hills, to make sure this man was dead. However, a mob from the city had rushed up to surround their saviour. Orion snarled, bitterly, then looked to the apocalyptic fires eating into the rocks and hills, carving out a crater. Night began to wash away the day, as the smoke from the conflagration eclipsed the sun entirely. From this pit, the flames seemed to roar and shriek with life of their own – the sights and sounds brought a crushing fretfulness into Orion's limbs and mind. There was something of the phoenix's soul or spirt in those arrows, and Orion had to kill the man who had them. Except that man was being ferried away by the fleeing citizens, and every legion in reserve would now be rampaging towards this site. Aside from it being next to impossible, there wouldn't be time to find the archer within the turmoil of panic and confusion – and he could hardly seek out the archer whilst wearing Dytrentian shackles.

Whoever this archer was, he had just saved the people of Eitimovel, giving them the time needed to flee, but at far too impossible a cost as far as Orion was concerned. Orion made to move, to get out of the city and flee as well. He would find the archer again, he vowed, if the archer was to survive his wounds, and put this unnatural entity down for good.

The Present...

Salt in the air was something Orion relished, having grown up far from the coast and in muggy heat. The cold breath of waves rolled out beyond their limits against the rocks to meet him, as if to weigh his presence. With each step over jagged outcroppings, tiny runnels filled and then receded under his boots. Miniature kingdoms within the countless pools and caves played out their natural lives; fleets of minute fish, sullen looking octopi, and many types of crabs getting on with their day.

This whole coastline, along the edge of Fohalin, the sliver of land which made up the country landlocking Bravenasil from the ocean, was built of welcoming stretches of warm sand, ordained by walls of rock, creating a regal tiara-like arc, only blighted by the Fohalin people's attempt to carve a port-city into it. Fohalin proper, however was comprised predominately of hundreds of small islands just off the coast of The Mane, making it one of the most opulent countries in all of The Mane as it brought in so many trade vessels.

"Chief? Sir? Which is it you prefer?" A watery, smooth tone broke over the waves.

Orion turned to his right, planted his spear down against the rocks, and grinned. "Ha! Ori will suffice. Give someone a title, and it comes with a desk." He marched over the jagged outcroppings with ease and clasped hands with Ivor Florakis, a member of the Flint Castle, and a merman.

The hybrid of human and marine animal, stood on his sleek shark-tail, coral-green with faded orange stripes, moulding organically into a human torso wearing luminescent layered armour. Pulses of green light swam around the hard shell-like attire, diffusing into white. Ivor's skin was pale, almost translucent, with veins, red and blue, and pale gold showing more vividly than in a human. The latter dedicated to moving and storing natural light, absorbed whenever possible, and feeding it into his skin whenever needed, to ensure good health in a world were sunlight could be reduced or even non-existent. Triangular teeth filled his mouth in a several rows, like a shark, with thin blonde hair covering his head. From the centre of Ivor's back rose an arch with a cartilage fin.

Merperson's aquatic biology took on many different forms, Ivor's human anatomy blended with that of sharks, his own species known for making excellent hunters and warriors as a result.

"Managed to shake Luci, then?" Ivor cast a glance past Orion.

"Well, we received an invitation from Fielder, to help hunt down a dominator," Orion began. Had Ivor eyebrows, he would have raised them, but his dark, glimmering eyes widened. "Did it as a favour for him, and for Luci too." Orion broke into a sly grin. "Luci slew the beast – it was maddening, I have to say. Felt less like a hunt and more like battle, but she got it. Not, however without injury." Ivor's face fell at that. "She's okay, though, recovering with the Scared Foresters, and loving it, I have to say. They've made her an honorary member and are grafting a prosthetic arm for her... The bugger bit her bow arm off. She had to draw the bow with her teeth – lost her front teeth in the process but nailed the bear..." Orion cackled rubbing his less well-kept beard.

158

"That woman is magnificent, Ori. She's come so far and done so well, for the Castle, us, and well, the natural order. You did a great thing rescuing her from that pit."

"It was duty, plain and simple. People don't think like we do. That syndicate, those pirates, had made her and the others into something outside of the natural order. I did what was necessary to fix that."

"Ha! You have a much clearer perspective on life than anyone I've met," Ivor added.

Whilst the Flint Castle had long ago banned members from hunting humanoids, such as merpersons, centaurs, manticore, sphinxes, and so on, and in time allowed them to join the ranks, it was Orion as Chair who pressed for reparations to be given to these groups, and who cut down any remaining prejudice.

"Well, I can't say that. Don't know how I feel about undead, however. I mean, the reanimates and such are unnatural, yes, but vampires? Should anyone really be overlooked by death?"

"Some religions argue that death is in fact unnatural, you know?"

"I don't know. Anyway, how is our plan coming along, Ivor?" The merman rose up straighter on his tail, sitting a foot taller than

Orion. From crown to tail Ivor was at least eight feet in length, and the melding of human into shark was so elegantly performed by natural laws that Orion was in awe of Ivor's figure, and a tad envious.

"Grand. We leaked the information about the vampire throughout the islands in the south... And I think we have interest. A rogue, or freelancer was seen taking a ship up here," Ivor spoke, his watery tones heating up.

The merpersons residing around the coasts of Fohalin had no love for the people of its myriad islands, or even the pirates further down the coast. It was not so long ago that Ivor's kind were still being hunted, if not persecuted, and Orion had known from the start that Ivor would be on board to help him draw out the Phoenix Archer, even if it required a great amount of collateral damage to the citizens residing within Fohalin.

For some time, Orion had known, through Ivor and other merperson members, of a wicked species of typhon residing to the east of Fohalin. If knowledge of this beast became known, it would destroy Fohalin's economy – no captain or merchant would risk losing ships. Given typhons were next to invulnerable, the governors of Fohalin captured a vampire, and held it in chains in the belly of a galleon which constantly patrolled the eastern perimeter of Fohalin, the deathly aura of the vampire keeping the beast at bay, and trade pouring in.

"I'm surprised they never asked you to slay the beast," Ivor inquired.

Orion chuckled. "Why would they? I'd cost them a fortune, and they've found a cheaper, easier solution. Besides, it wouldn't matter if I slew it. It'd be too high profile an affair to go unnoticed, and even the memory of such a beast would be enough to deter traders."

"Typical government; spend as little as you can and hope for the best results."

"Greed. It comes with the territory, unfortunately."

"Well, this freelancer, will take care of the vampire, and the beast will return. Are you _sure_ it will draw this archer out?"

"Well, worst case, I add to my accolades slaying the typhon. No. He'll show. He couldn't let the people of Eitimovel suffer at the hands of the Dytrentians, and he didn't even know them. He won't allow so much death or destruction to befall the people of Fohalin if he can do something to stop it."

"What about us?" Ivor added, looking up the coast, across the gold sands, the steely rocks, towards where the first of many islands sat ethereally in the distance.

"Stay away. I can take the archer, and I don't want any old prejudices coming back. If anyone sees merpersons in the waters, they'll not hesitate to accuse your people of this."

With a thoughtful look, Ivor considered this. "Alright. But this archer, he took down Bailey, didn't he?"

"So, he's smarter than a brute like Bailey. Bailey was all natural talent. He never had to struggle for anything in his life, so he was over-confident. Besides, I *need* to be the one to do this." Orion took the long wrap of cloth from off his shoulder and held it out.

Ivor's dark eyes widened with awe and fear. "Gods, Orion, I didn't think it was real. Are you sure that's it."

"Certain. You know how many times I've tried to draw this to make sure?" The Crowned Bow, or Vainglory Bow, only capable of being drawn on 'worthy' targets. "This is the perfect bow for people like us. It tells us what can raise our standing and what must be extinguished. The Phoenix Archer, he defiles the natural world, and when this bow draws on him, I will be proven right."

Chapter VI – The Vainglory Typhon

Gwillim Prothero's hatred for vampires infested his psyche.

Leather gloves, dark green to match the leather face wrap, helped against the psychodynamic symptoms: imagined chest pains, a burning throat. Gwillim was self-aware enough to understand how irrational this was but needed the comfort of his attire and cleanliness routines, nonetheless.

Slipping aboard the tiny vessel unseen was simple for the former Fang-Stalker Guild member. The more militant of the vampire slaying Guild would have required him to dispatch the whole crew – anyone who was in close contact with the abomination. Such militantism was why he left. Rather, Gwillim ensured no harm came to the crew, given most were unaware of what was being smuggled.

Why they were smuggling a vampire, Gwillim couldn't say; some hunted them for sport; some older vampires held centuries of knowledge and were a treasure trove for academics. Given the emaciation of this beast, it looked to have been kept in chains for decades. Gwillim had seen countless vampires, but never one so decrepit, closer in appearance to an aged corpse.

Almost colourless eyes rolled up from sunken holes to meet Gwillim. He almost had to look away, as if the disgust of this creature could be transmitted through eye contact. A pathetic wheeze fell from its maw.

Three Days Earlier...

The beast of a ship took Ksenia's heart once more; an unyielding grasp threatening to take more decades from her: The Daemon Flamingo.

Sweeping, pitch black wings ran along either side of the body, arcing upwards. Three huge masts ran down the centre of the ship, glowing pink sails furled. To the rear, the wood was carved into a conflagration of tail feathers, glowing, and pulsing between shades of orange. The prow was shaped into a blunt, hooked beak for ramming other ships, and its gait told of how it could comfortably hold a crew of seventy, and a horde of riches.

This legend was sheltered in the port of Nauberta, a pirate city. Besieging the horizon were uncountable flags, fronting the vast, murky green mountains. Brothels fell over temples, and taverns overflowed into administrative buildings. Lounging along jetties, was every known variation of sentient species, everyone was armed and ostentatiously ordained in pilfered treasures. It was exactly as Ksenia had left it; unordered and carefree. Alejandro moved warily; his face wrap up to match his guard. To him everyone was a dangerous, unpredictable predator.

They moved on from the docks, navigating tight, overcrowded streets, every lane thick with revellers and whores.

"Like navigating the Abyssal Labyrinth," Alejandro muttered. "Only we're not going to be rewarded with dark magic if we survive."

"This was your idea," Ksenia replied stepping over a prostrate drunk.

"I encountered a thirty-member gorilla troop once; had to sit still for an hour, staring into the ground, whilst they drank from the same river. *That* was less stressful."

"I trust your judgment, Alejandro," Ksenia began, wincing as she used his name, worried it conveyed too much. His good eyebrow rose in curiosity, and he stopped walking. Ksenia sighed. "This is stupid. You don't see a bear trap and stick your foot into it, and that is exactly what you're doing."

"And what do you propose? If only every fight could be on our terms, Ksenia. In fact, we're lucky Brencis sold Orion out, and that puts us in a better position than we would have been. We know Orion will be there, somewhere, hunting me."

Ksenia swallowed at the word 'hunting', feeling a chill. "I'm still annoyed we let Brencis walk." They had had many iterations of this conversation over the past week; however she knew deep down, they had to do something.

"The Castle will figure it out... And get him."

Naturally the Fohalin government was out of the question. They would likely kill or throw her and Alejandro into a cell for knowing about the typhon, whilst gambling that Orion would become professionally obligated to act.

And as if a lack of oversight for the protection of Fohalin citizens wasn't enough, Typhons, like any gigantic sea beast did not fear phoenixes. To Ksenia's knowledge these were the only animals the world over not to. Alejandro believed this was because the ocean was not a phoenix's domain, and simply, had no business being there. They couldn't drown or have their fire doused, but the constant battle between untameable fire and unlimited oceanic turbulence would be exceptionally painful for the animal. Phoenixes were exclusively land animals, and Typhons had no reason to fear something that would never infringe on their domain.

Finally, Ksenia came to the Scrappin' Batterin', and swept in as if she belonged there.

Mismatched and crowded tables were scattered throughout. On some there were dancers, on others drinking games. Tavern staff deftly glided by with more tankards than looked possible to carry. A stage was built into the far wall, with dancers, dressed as women, but Ksenia knew enough to know they weren't.

"Copper for a drink," a voice whispered. Ksenia turned to see Alejandro frozen, eyes locked in exasperation. A shadowy figure, a head smaller than the archer lurked behind him, with a sleek dagger pointed into the side of his neck.

"Fredricka van der Veer," Ksenia laughed. "Must be early. You're still standing... And coherent."

Fredricka withdrew the dagger and pressed past Alejandro. "The Lady of Feathers coming back to the nest? Oh, the fun we used to have. And the seas have only gotten richer since you left!" She playfully thrust and parried with her dagger about Ksenia's frame before stepping back and throwing an arm over Alejandro's shoulders – much to his well-hidden disgust.

Ksenia's old associate had braided rust-red hair and emerald eyes. A nasty stab scar bore into her left cheek, marred almost black from residual black powder. However, her elven ears were artificial at the pointed tips, emerald coloured metal were flesh and cartilage should've been – self-inflicted, for decoration's sake. Ksenia recalled the drunken discussion in which they both thought it would be a brilliant idea. A burst of heat surged into the darkened void that had been left when Ksenia left the Daemon Flamingo.

"If I came back, you'd have to actually work." Ksenia leaped forward and embraced her old friend. Blunt handles from pistols and daggers pressed into her.

"I'm getting my hopes up, Ksenia, that you – and this sullen lookin' thing – will be coming back aboard."

Ksenia had momentarily forgotten about Alejandro. "Oh, this is Alejandro Zaragosa, a good friend of mine – I've known him longer that you miscreants."

"Don't make me jealous, dear, I have too many sharp edges about me person," Fredricka laughed. She looked to the face wrap. "How mysterious."

"Best not," Ksenia jumped in. "We need to see the captain."

Any sphinxes' features could cover any species of the animals incorporated into the human form. Captain Egil Pearce, a bipedal fusion of man and cat, was covered in murky gold fur, with grey rings simmering underneath. From his back, folded, hiding their size and magnificence, were wings, largely white due to a condition known as leucism in which the colour pigments failed to manifest. Yet, this regal banner was streaked with warm pink in places. His face was tanned, soft skinned with glowing brown eyes, a small flat nose, and sharp mouth. When Egil grinned, eagerly upon seeing Ksenia, fangs protruded. A tail with a dirty gold bush at the end swirled and danced restlessly from behind his formidable frame.

"Has the grand raptor of the seas come back to the Daemon, to grace its deck once more with the blood of our enemies!?" Egil cracked a fist on his table, then rose to his full seven feet.

The room was a private den. Small tables littered the floor, with cushions scattered throughout. The scents of various narcotics and spirits created an almost tangible force.

Ksenia didn't want to get her old mentor's hopes up. It was enough, marring this reunion, asking for a favour. "Egil, you resplendent rascal." She couldn't, however, help but throw her arms about the giant's rock-dense frame. Scratchy barbs met her exposed skin, and face.

"I... *We* need your help," she began, remembering Alejandro.

"And what can this servant of the oceans do for you?" Ksenia felt the hairs on her arms tingle at the *hiss* in Egil's voice which ran along the first syllable of her name. He moved past her to Alejandro, the glaring inconstancy in the room. Tall, lean, and smouldering, with arms folded. Ksenia was sure he was doing his best not to seem defensive, however, pirates were notoriously erratic. "Who is this... Volcano?" Egil placed his hands on both Alejandro's shoulders, narrowing his gaze on the stranger.

"Alejandro Zaragosa, a dear friend of mine," she began.

"Oh, the adventuring archer you spoke so, *affectionately*, of when you first graced my deck..."

Ksenia's pulse threatened to leap out of her neck. "Yes, well, yes... We need your help."

"I think he's hiding something," Egil cackled, looking around to the various members of his crew. He gingerly tugged at the wrap on Alejandro's face with an onyx-grey talon, before pulling it away.

Egil gasped, theatrically, with irony before stepping back. "Magnificent! What glorious scars." The room fell to silence. "And..." He leaned in close to the glassy scars, sniffing. "You have the heat of something ferocious, eternal... A perpetual force of nature *imbued* in those scars."

Alejandro cracked a half smile, and in his signature slur, with the tenor of a hammer striking hot metal said, "Meow."

There was silence, lead heavy. Then Egil roared in laughter. He clapped Alejandro's shoulder and turned back to Ksenia. "I love him." He looked back to Alejandro. "Forgive my intrusiveness, but strangers to my ship, any ship, must be dressed down to see their true selves. *Even* if someone as trusted as The Lady of Feathers is vouching for you."

"No offense taken, captain," Alejandro continued, half-smirking. "I didn't know what to expect either." Egil laughed sharply. "But, not to force the issue, I need your help. And I can't compensate you..."

"Hmm, how about a few of those fancy arrows, I can feel the heat from, humming away, in your quiver?" Egil gestured to the wrapped back quiver holding Alejandro's bow and arrows.

Alejandro raised his good eyebrow. "I can't do that…"

"I'm joking, I'm joking." He looked to Ksenia. "All The Lady of Feathers must do to have my help, is ask… Though I do get to draw you. No! Sculpt. No! Paint. Watercolours. No! Oils."

The Present…

It came as a surprise to Gwillim when something blunt caught him on the back of the head. The interior of the hold grew dark, and over him, was the lean figure of a man in a face wrap.

 Was it supposed to be so easy? Ksenia thought. The Daemon Flamingo had rolled along the smooth waters; a cloaking spell manifested from ship's bow. Once the small, tatty vessel was in sight, one of Egil's mages cast a portals spell transporting herself and Alejandro aboard it. Major magic was always frightening, but Ksenia was so eager to get aboard this unmarked vessel and secure the vampire, it hardly fazed her.

An explosion tore open the bulkhead behind them. Splitters whipped into Ksenia, and she fell. The too familiar roar of water struck her next, and suddenly icy torrents engulfed her lower body.

"Damnation!" Alejandro was shouting.

Screaming from above fell down into the hold as the crew above panicked. Another thunderous blast shook the ship and the screaming intensified.

"Vampires can't drown," Ksenia yelled over the roaring, rising waters. "What are you doing?"

Smashing the lock on the cell, Alejandro moved inside. "I know. But the sunlight will vaporise it before it can sink deep enough!"

Ksenia cursed herself scrabbling through the straining weight of the water. It was all so familiar, rushing to get hold of anything valuable, whilst the ocean threatened to swallow her.

However, a greater explosion tore her from the cell, away from Alejandro. Something pulled her back, her waist, arms, and legs seized by an invisible force. Pannels and shreds of wood surrounded Ksenia like a tornado, two halves of the ship sank, spilling crates, debris, and bodies. A mast had fallen over and was tangled between the halves, as if trying in vain to keep the ship together.

Where was Alejandro? Ksenia was fretting, fighting the sucking motion of the sinking ship. She fought, pulling herself up, and up, through the debris field. As she broke the surface the screeching of the Daemon Flamingo's guns rolled over her. Ksenia whirled around to see another ship behind her, twofold bigger than the Flamingo, ripping through the ocean.

Orion! It had to be him.

She saw what had made short work of the prison ship; sleek hooks on teethers launched through the air at the Flamingo – made for hunting large oceanic animals. A shielding on the Flamingo swatted them away, though barely.

Ksenia splashed over the upset of the water caused by the Flamingo, towards its black winged hull. Another volley took, shrieking, to the sky, towards Orion's flagship.

A rope ladder fell to dangle into the water, and Ksenia grasped at it, coarse, wet hemp cutting into her palms. She spat water and pulled herself up. As the masts with their vivid pink sails wavered under the sky, Ksenia saw ethereal whisps forming, darkening. A gale was developing, pushing her to the side as she climbed. Egil was making use of his storm-surge device, a magical relic which could alter the weather.

At the top Fredericka pulled Ksenia over onto the deck. All about them pirates ran purposefully. In the masts, archers loosed hot, pink, burning arrows. Surrounding the ship, arcs of lightning broke out as enemy shot and hooks were repulsed.

Finally, having regrouped, Ksenia thought, *Where's Alejandro?* Panic seized her gut. She turned to look over the railing, begging the Gods that he'd be there, right behind her. But the Flamingo was roaring forward, Egil ready to smash Orion's flagship. Winds generated from the weather magic launched the Flamingo like an arrow.

A hook breached the shield, narrowly missing the first mast, before shattering through the centre mast and crashing through the deck. Ksenia was pulled to her right as the mechanisations aboard the flagship began to real in the hook. The Flamingo's momentum was stolen, and the mighty ship was forcefully pulled side on. Ksenia yelped and she and Fredricka slipped and rolled across the deck. The centre mast threatened to fall. Tipping with the tilt of the ship, several archers tumbled overboard.

"Prepare for boarding action!" Fredricka was crying at those around them, clambering back to her feet. Ksenia pulled herself up. If Orion was going to pull the Flamingo in like prey, Ksenia knew Egil would seize the opportunity to meet him halfway. Pirates all around her cheered and roared as they grasped at netting, rails, and anything else to avoid tumbling overboard.

Taking hold of the base of the centre mast, Ksenia looked ahead to the colossal flagship. There had to be double the number of hands the Flamingo had, with a security force too, and Orion and Luciana to boot. Her pirates were going to really enjoy themselves, and where it not for Alejandro being missing, she'd have smirked in anticipation.

In an attempt to overshadow her concern, from the tempest between the ships, from the depths came the bronze and golden scales of the Vainglory Typhon. Its curved head caught the reel from the hook lodged in the Flamingo, sheering it apart like a rotten twig. Tension from the reel however sent the hook's-half whipping down into the sea with enough speed to illicit thunder.

Towering hundreds of feet into the sky, the giant snake flexed its maw, fangs large enough to impale either ship, flaring. Hoods at either side of its head broke out, and its bronze eyes, cut through with blood red, turned looking towards the Flamingo, before glaring at the flagship. Among the golden scales, bronze scales, fading into lighter shades of brown, seemed to slither around the animal's body as is it was being constructed by a smaller snake.

"You didn't get the vampire, then?" Fredricka shouted above the crashing waters falling from the towering beast. She was grinning, her hair matted down by the wet, the emerald points of her ears glinting through the mess.

The sunlight had slain the vampire. Ksenia had to admit she felt relief for whoever it had been. Now at peace, no longer in agony.

The typhon arched back, energy snapping from its hood, altering the atmosphere. Its size ensured the space between the ships descended into a hurricane force storm in seconds. Waves hundreds of feet tall came up from under the Flamingo. Ksenia gripped the rails under the centre mast even harder. Her feet left the deck, and cries rose around her. Several pirates flailed past. As the Flamingo was thrown to the left, the silhouette of another ship appeared through a wave rising over the Flamingo. It grew in profile as it was launched towards them.

Fohalin was predominantly a nation of islands, and Alejandro had no idea which one he could possibly have washed up on.

The sand was course, scratching the good side of his face. Rising to his knees his body spasmed. Violently, Alejandro began vomiting seawater. This wasn't the first time he'd drowned, and he knew the routine, letting his body work. He spat one final mouthful of tangy seawater and sat on his knees. Before him was a tangle of rainforest and rocks breaking out from the sand.

So long as he was moving Alejandro knew he was good. Of course, the pain was doing its darndest to be felt through the better side of his body; ribs shrieking, lower-back wincing, and his shoulder twinging with every movement.

Checking his leather bow-sheath was still fixed on his back, Alejandro moved into the cover of the rainforest. Where was Ksenia? The Flamingo? Orion? A bolt of darkening concern shot through his gut at the latter. Even in prime condition, Alejandro was concerned about his chances.

Whispering through the soft breeze, beckoning him into the rainforest, were recognisable echoes. Fighting. He moved forward through knee-high foliage. The heat became muggy, and Alejandro would have given anything for a cool breath of air to sooth his dry mouth. He took a swing from a waterskin still on his belt. Pure bliss poured down into his belly. His head settled, and breathing became less arduous.

He would have seen the gorge; however, something stole his focus, and Alejandro launched himself to the right. A battering ram crashed into his gut, low and left, breaking the leather armour, and breeching his silk undergarment. Searing heat followed, slicing deep. Alejandro found himself slipping, clipping an arm on a rocky outcrop, cracking a leg on another, trying desperately to stay on his back. If he rolled, the arrow in his gut would do more damage.

Alejandro met a stream, feet first. Pulling himself up, another bite from the embedded arrow almost doubled him over. His left leg refused to move, seized by dull agony, and he hopped frantically. He clutched the arrow jutting out his gut, the flights on it cutting into his hand. Had he not seen the blood pour from his fingers, he'd have never noticed; raze pheasant feathers, a vicious little game bird found on The Sigel.

Never had Ksenia felt so powerless under the ferocity of nature. Between flashes of bright blue, hot white, and sudden abyssal darkness, the whole of the Daemon Flamingo had been taken into the clutches of a hurricane.

The Flamingo had been tossed into the shoals of a small island, leaning wounded against a reef of sand and rocks. The two remaining masts were tilting, gaping splintered gashes along their lengths. The prow was smashed to one side like a broken in nose. Along the right side of the ship, the battery of cannons still functioned, crewed by bloodied die-hards, launching shot after shot over the golden sands and bloody waters. Their target was the flagship, moored in a similarly wounded predicament less than a hundred yards away; its prow was held high into the air, the body and gut of the ship having carved a channel through the reef into the island's base.

The no-man's land between was rife with pools of pink froth, where the ocean waves broke over bodies; pirates and the those of Orion's hired security. Between the dead and dying, cutlass wielding pirates leapt upon armoured mercenaries, thrusting, and parrying with their own spears and axes. Within this turmoil, Captain Egil Pearce parried, slashed, and eviscerated with a sabre as dense as any mountain, and as manageable as a feather. The brute of muscle and fur wasn't against cracking knees and caving in armour with kicks five times as strong as any human's. His wings were arced high and wide, magic playing out a conflagration across the feathers.

A hasty arrow went low and took a coral-green-armoured mercenary in the leg. Ksenia followed up with another to the throat. A crack of black powder igniting filled the air with more acrid smoke as Fredricka blasted with utter glee into the advancing enemy. She dropped the pistol and drew another, taking another mercenary down in a flare of fire. Behind them a pirate's apprentice picked up the discarded weapons and hurriedly reloaded them.

The pair were cornered on the outcropping of rocks by the front of the Flamingo. Together they were holding off attackers looking to breech the hull and silence the guns – the Flamingo's last advantage.

Ksenia nocked and loosed arrow after arrow from her hip quiver, her matted down dress of exotic bird, griffin, and dragon feathers throwing the terror colours of blood, fire, and the abyss against the greenish corals of advancing enemies' armour.

Several of the sleek warriors had arrows embedded in their torso plating, or sticking out of their sides and extremities, but advanced, nonetheless. With the rocks, as sharp as any blade, footing was practically impossible. In tandem with the wet, the attackers had a choice of focusing on balance or trying to lash out with their tall spears.

Their only saving grace was that the typhon had disappeared. Ksenia needed to get out of this corner, break the enemies back and get searching for Alejandro. She knew currents and storms, and knew he had to have been washed up somewhere close by. Desperate energy and uncertainty were wavering through her arms and blunting the effort she threw into stretching her back muscles to draw her bow.

A lean figure crashed down to Alejandro's left, a shadow of lithe energy moving faster than he could. Before Alejandro could turn, or find his flint dagger, the world blurred. The sloshing water was about his head, running over his limbs.

"A crusade, vindicated," a voice hissed. Orion Aldenberg.

A metal boot came down on Alejandro's chest, glints of brownish behemoth bone fused within the steel. "The Phoenix Archer! My greatest game. I almost thought you'd perished at Eitimovel. Almost gave up looking for you." With lightning speed Orion ripped the arrow from Alejandro's gut. He barked in aguish. "Eighteen years, this has been my longest stalk."

Refusing to look weak, Alejandro stammered, "I'd have moved on..." He looked up at the figure, framed in the sunlight breaking through the tangled branches; a ragged beard sat untidily under dark eyes and bald head. A tight armoured attire had been tailored to the lithe frame; golden coloured metals infused with the jewel like hue of behemoth bone to create an almost indestructible attire. The insignia of the Flint Castle was glaring at him from the breastplate in ivory; an arrow crossing a spear, with the head of a typhon in the top corner, the head of a pheasant in the right corner, the crested head of a lizard in the bottom corner, and the head of a hyena in the left corner.

Alejandro grinned, teeth awash in blood. He went for his flint dagger with his left arm, a feint, and Orion stabbed down with the arrow, boring into Alejandro's shoulder, his bad shoulder, with little feeling in it. Moving with his right hand, Alejandro caught the hilt of his dagger and thrust the weapon into Orion's waist, between armour joints.

Reeling, Orion leapt back. Alejandro pulled the arrow from his shoulder. He thrust the arrow at Orion's neck, straining anguish wracking his whole right side, harrying his attack. There was enough strength for Alejandro to regain his footing, however Orion batted the arrow away. They locked eyes, and Alejandro saw the hunger of a wild cat smouldering in the dark. Using the left side of his face, Alejandro headbutted the hunter, feeling little of the crack, but enough heat to know he'd split Orion's nose. Unfazed, Orion brought a fist around and cracked Alejandro on his right side. Stunned, his whole right side finally giving up. With his bloody left hand, he caught Orion by the collar and pulled him down into the all-consuming brush. Alejandro rolled away, painfully over tangles of tree roots. To his right he caught the vivid red of a root adder and grabbed it. He grasped the confused animal under its pebbled head and threw it towards Orion. Orion caught the serpent. It wasn't fatally venomous, however it looked enough like its killer cousin to hold Orion for a moment.

Alejandro closed the gap, scooped up a rock and clattered the hunter on the head. Orion dropped the serpent. With his other hand Alejandro grasped the open side of Orion's face, stabbing his thumb into an eye – *enchanted prosthetic!* Orion roared, more in anger than pain and jumped back, a hand over his eye, the other awash in blood, blinding him.

Dark hues caught Alejandro's eyes, breaking out from the brush. Orion's bow! Through stabbing pains, Alejandro reached for it, catching the grip. As he rolled away, the leather strap of his bow sheath snapped, spilling his own bow out, disappearing among the foliage. Alejandro scrambled around the base of a wide tree. Panting, chest fluttering in agony, Alejandro pulled his bow-sheath around, wincing as he noticed the gap where his bow should be. He pulled the wooden tube of arrows free, and with bloodied fingers fumbled with the nocks to get as many out as possible.

"I once had to go fists to talons with an ash lion!" Came a roar from somewhere behind him. "Knocked its fangs out, but not before it took my eye! An eye you just took!" A rough cackling rose. "Five continents – and even more ocean. How little of the world could we ever hope to see in our lifetime? And yet, I found you *twice*! You know me, of course. Chief Hunter, Orion Aldenberg of the Flint Castle. Top of your own hunting list. But we first met, at the crucible which made you the man you are today!"

Eitimovel... The blur of angry orange flames and arcs of abyssal black smoke came back to Alejandro. The scent of burning meat assaulted his nose, choking him, the cries boring into his ears with crippling aguish.

"I watched you wield a power which should never have been anyone's. You took it and committed a wretched transgression! Saving my people, through such a means was a wicked act!"

One of the citizens I saved... The Gods love irony... Alejandro recalled a crack Ksenia had made about gratitude, and the thought made him smirk.

"Nature can never be tamed! It's ruthlessness, its savagery is what can make us champions, as we strive against it. Iron sharpens iron, and nature gives us the means to become greater. Without it, we're nothing, left to die out! But you stole its power! Who are you to try and supplant nature!? You're an abomination, and that bow you hold says so! Heard of the Crowned Bow? Of course, you have. What self-respecting archer hasn't? Nature's own bow, to cull what must be culled!"

As Orion said the name, Alejandro's fingers found the scratches, the tallies marked into the riser. Four of them. And he was apparently on his way to becoming the fifth.

Or it only draws on target's worthy of being hunted... Alejandro came close to shouting back. *Read the lore.*

Now he wondered if the bow would even draw on Orion. It had to. It drew on him after all, and he was hardly the predator Orion was. He fixed his quiver of covered phoenix arrows to his thy, fitting as many of his regular arrows as he could into the spare funnel.

Alejandro dared a glance beyond the tree. Every shade of green melded and glistened back though a murky abyss. He couldn't see Orion. But a soft click had him ducking back, and the crack of a bolt ricocheting sent bark biting into his face.

Where did he get a crossbow from? Alejandro dared another glance. He leaned about further on his haunches, knowing he was being reckless.

There! The gold glints broke through the foliage and Alejandro didn't hesitate. He raised the bow but was too slow. Orion's right arm was up, the spread-wings of a crossbow fitted to his forearm flaring. A bolt whipped by Alejandro, between him and the tree. A deliberately placed shot, forcing him out into the open. Alejandro hardly had the time to draw the bow before Orion's crossbow had automatically loaded another bolt. Instead, Alejandro dared to do something potentially stupid. He snatched the cover from the phoenix arrows to let the heat loose, and to see what denizens called this rainforest home.

Orion loosed another bolt, catching Alejandro in the chest. With the breath stolen from him, Alejandro staggered back until he crashed against a tree. Tepid blood filled his mouth. He heard himself wheezing, knowing too well that a hunter like Orion was never going to miss an open lung-shot.

His coughing was thundered over by the sudden surge of animal life. Countless species raced between and behind the dualling pair. Flightless birds with elongated necks ripped through the vines and ferns. Big cats moaned, their dark-orange and brown coats barely visible as they tore through the foliage. Then came the gorillas. Huge, black, and indigo edifices clambered through with all the power of a landslide.

The scene was magnificent, and he thought if this is the last sight he had to see, it was more than he could ask for.

Between the blurs and stampeding beasts, Orion ducked and tumbled. The hunter was too canny, however. He'd likely been here before, and knew precisely when to leap, and where to step. Still, Alejandro saw his moment. But so did Orion.

He raised his crossbow and loosed a bolt. At the last second a gemsbox whipped by close enough to throw him off balance. The bolt went wide, past Alejandro.

The last horned cattle animal cleared the scene, the rainforest obliterated. Every fibre of plant crushed to pulp. Up to a height of ten feet, trees were bare of branches, and their barks stripped clean of vines and ivy.

Orion took aim with his crossbow but hesitated. Fifteen yards away was Alejandro, holding the Crowned bow on him... At full draw.

Mud caked blood was smeared over Orion's face, sweat pouring over it. Orion muttered, "That's something..."

They loosed at the same time.

This was not a fight the crew of the Daemon Flamingo could win.

Skirmishes, raids; dirty, fast, hit and runs were what they excelled at. But here, on an open battlefield, not only were they outnumbered, but out matched in tactics. Orion's security was a mercenary company, Tidal Charioteers. These mercenaries had formed up into ranks, and surrounded the pirates, pinning them with their backs to the Flamingo.

During the tempest three of the Flamingo's mages were killed when the boulder sized relic, used for weather control, broke from its mounts, crushing them. Two more had their chest blown through by loose magical energy, and the last was in a coma from being thrown around.

On the left flank, Ksenia and Fredricka were taking more than the brunt of the enemy pincer movement. In part, the rocks, and their inability to provide solid footing was keeping them alive against superior numbers. The rest was Ksenia's skill with her bow.

The Flamingo's guns were still doing damage to the Tidal Charioteers. Half their force was pinned down in no man's land, behind their main force.

A spearhead drew hot blood through Ksenia's thigh. She loosed an arrow wide and hit the soldier on his left, tumbling him. She nocked another and sent it into a faceplate. At the base of the rocks, armoured bodies, pinned with arrows were now giving Tidal Charioteers better footing. They were getting closer and into better thrusting range. Ksenia, still fretting over Alejandro, was desperate to get into the rainforest. Here and now, though, it was constant shooting down attackers, keeping her gunners safe – and she knew with chilling certainty, that that was going to fail sooner rather than later.

Then, the colossus that was Orion's flagship erupted into an inferno. A swirl of shrieking orange poured into the sky, mushrooming out into blindingly white flame. Ksenia's eyes stung. She pulled her eyes away until the flare dulled. From the epicentre came jagged fissures breaking through the sand and rock, oozing molten rage. And from these gashes came talons of inky smoke.

Then the slaughter began.

Tidal Charioteers, stuck behind the Flamingo's cannons rushed the no-man's land to escape the hunting fires. None made it as the fissures combusted soldiers, superheated smoke searing to ash the lungs of others. A wave of shimmering, howling heat poured out from the impact point purging any remaining trace of the mercenaries. The fires from the blast rose upwards into the sky to leave only a blackened, glistening crater were once the gigantic flagship sat.

In a panic the remaining Tidal Charioteers broke ranks and fled, in whichever direction they could – into the rainforest, others into the ocean. The pirates did not relent, and where they could, cut down the retreating mercenaries.

Eyes streaming, Ksenia looked over to the far left, the edge of the rainforest, were a figure stood, bow in hand, then collapsed. The pirates all around her were cheering, enraptured by the force of nature they had witnessed. Ksenia didn't join them, she only wanted Alejandro back. So Ksenia clambered down the slippery, jagged rocks, over the blood-slickened dead and bolted as fast as she could ever remember running across the sand.

She slid do a stop by the still body. It was Alejandro of course, his leviathan face-wrap up on. Ksenia pulled it away and grasped his bloodied, grimy face; one side bare and smeared with glassy burn scars, the other bristling with black hair. She held her ear to his lips. He was wheezing, barely. Ksenia's hands met her clammy face, and she wiped away tears and sweat. She had lost him once before, decades ago when she chose the Daemon Flamingo, and he had chosen to pursue phoenixes.

Tremors rattled the sand and rocks beneath them, forcing Ksenia back into a rush. She almost tumbled, but Fredricka grasped her arm. Ksenia hadn't even noticed her. The tremors merged into one continuous quake, trees splitting and crashing down. Animal's shrieking rose up over the sound of the ground beneath them splitting and cracking.

"It's the typhon!" Fredricka shouted, managing to get to her feet. "It's constricting the island! Come on, Ksenia." They took hold of Alejandro under his arms. As the pair lumbered awkwardly over the trembling sands Egil came crashing down, caked in sand and blood. With one arm he threw Alejandro over a shoulder and barked at Ksenia and Fredricka to move. Even with the unconscious archer over his shoulder Egil's strides were huge, and his speed fierce. By contrast Ksenia was faltering and staggering like a drunk trying to dance along a railing. However, the typhon's attack was not without a measure of saving grace. The Flamingo had been shaken from its beached position, and the waves were rising rapidly – they had a way out.

The final leg had Ksenia wading through blood slickened waters, with bits of people bobbing by her. Fredricka helped her onto the rope ladder and saw her up over the rails.

As the boards vibrated and everything about her rattled, Ksenia could see several of the ships medical practitioners lifting Alejandro and moving him into the cover of one of the above deck cabins. She made to follow, catching the magnificence of Egil on the command deck howling out orders.

Before she followed Alejandro, Ksenia looked back towards the island, obscured by thick clouds of dust. From it rose the hooded maw of the typhon, silhouetted into inky black by the sun.

She paused, staring into the abyssal black shadow, a hand grasping the frame of the doorway. She wondered what it was that Alejandro first felt when he first encountered a phoenix. What was it what he saw, through the terror, and horror of the animal which no one else did?

I'll damn well ask him when he's awake, she thought determinedly, pushing herself into the medical cabin. Alejandro was going nowhere, Ksenia decided. The afterworld could wait.

Epilogue – Aldenberg's Panther

Two months after part six...

Evander Penrose sat in the muggy shade of an outdoor tavern, lemon-water to hand. Currently he was in the Wetsven capital, only fifty yards from the infamous Shroud Fastness. This bank held in its guts the wealth and secrets of the most notorious and affluent on not just The Sigel, but The Crown, and The Mane – rumours whispered that even the Dytrentian Empire had treasures and secrets buried there too.

He had been reflecting on the issues regarding the man his superiors had designated The Phoenix Archer. Evander had to admit that Alejandro was not the man he had thought. If he'd been a miscreant, then the mission would have been simpler. Instead, he had to sell to his superiors, that Alejandro was better as a potential asset to Maytoni. His knowledge could be crucial. And that knowledge was Alejandro's only advantage in his crusade against the Flint Castle, especially Orion Aldenberg.

As for that crusade, its outcome was one Evander was happy with. Not just because Orion was dead – his body recovered by Luciana Doran and interred within the Flint Castle – but because Alejandro survived the fight.

From intelligence gleaned through embassy agents, Luciana had not been present at the finale, having been wounded taking down a dominator. *Good mercy*, Evander had thought. Had she been there, Alejandro and Ksenia would be dead.

Officially, Orion Aldenberg had died defending a fishing trawler from pirates, not just any grimy, haggard band, but the crew of the legendary Daemon Flamingo – Evander, as much as he hated the sea, would have loved to have set eyes on that particular vessel.

Furthermore, there were rumours now of a vainglory typhon off the east of Fohalin. The government was denying it, stating any sightings were the result of 'magic tricks' played by the Daemon Flamingo in the hope to redirect any ships south into pirate territory.

A so-called vampire (Evander, like all Maytoni did not believe in vampires) being used to keep the beast at bay was an audacious, dangerous move, and inevitably it was going to go awry. But for Orion to bring a vainglory typhon into the fight, holding tens of thousands, even hundreds of thousands hostage, to draw The Phoenix Archer out, was megalomaniacal.

Orion was a complicated man; anti-slave, an advocate for sentience-species equality, but his perspective on deaths from the devastating actions of something like a typhon, as simply nature doing its thing was cold and too fatalistic for Evander's liking. It was a devious plan that Luciana would not have been happy with. She therefore had to have had no knowledge of it. Evander wasn't prepared to go far enough to envision Orion using the dominator hunt as way to incapacitate Luciana, confident that her wounds were a convenient coincidence. Afterall, Evander had mused, grimly, if anyone could put down a dominator, it would a beast like Lunciana Doran.

Oddly, Brencis Fong, treasurer to the Castle, was dead too, found dismembered, and with his throat torn out, in South Ceiho. It looked like a bear attack, only for the fact that the body had not been munched on – and there were no bears in South Ceiho. Adding to this, the expedition manager, Amdt Aakster, was currently missing.

Evander had a theory that Brencis had sold Orion out. As for Amdt Aakster, the man was a close confident of Orion's, who would follow any order given without question. They'd been brothers through the hunt, almost as close to him as Luciana had been. He must have known something about Orion's plan, and Luciana was looking for him. The thought made Evander shiver, though he wasn't feeling sorry for the former expedition manager. Evander had engaged mage's who wielded horror like a knight would a sword, and centaurs in full battle armour, even taken on odds well against himself and come out bloody and triumphant. But Luciana, she scared him.

A quake had unsettled the order of the Flint Castle. Its leader dead, a senior figure dead, and another senior figure in hiding – soon to be dead no doubt. Luciana Doran was now in charge and those empty posts had been filled. Intelligence had come to Evander for a few weeks in the aftermath of Orion's death, confirming further deaths of various Castle members, all Orion loyalists – including a merman, Ivor Florakis. Luciana was enraged alright. She'd been exercising her frustrations over Orion's betrayal, whilst conveniently purging anyone who might try to oust her in favour of another Orion Aldenberg.

Evander felt sorry for her. To have someone who was kin, who had saved her life, brought her back into the civilised world, keep such a dark secret and enact such a dark scheme, would obliterate her reality, and crush her soul. In a way, though Evander hated everything the Flint Castle stood for, he secretly hoped Luciana could come back from this.

Where the Castle was going next, he couldn't say. However, Evander had hardly put the incident down when all Chasm was threatening to open up under his beloved Maytoni.

The past month for Evander Penrose had been far from great. A contrived war with Maytoni's neighbours, the Xellcarrians, brought on by the arrogance and entitlement of a self-declared prince, had left him feeling hollow and bitter. Prince Darren Sharrow of Maytoni had shot down a griffin within what the Xellcarrians claimed was their sea border. The prince denied it, despite the fact the Xellcarrians had no reason lie. Given Xellcarrians didn't only see the animals as divine, aspects of their gods', but worshiped them too, hostility was a certainty.

The War of the Feathers it had been called, and its history was that of a week, and one bloody avoidable battle. Xellcarrian forces attempted to annex Maytoni's Mayne Peninsula, holding it and the people there, hostage, until the prince was handed over.

Evander, five other Summiteers and a regular army group were the only forces present to stonewall the surprise attack. As far as Evander was concerned, nobody won, though officially, Maytoni forces had broken an army of superior numbers.

For his discernment, and actions in attempting to deescalate the conflict, and keeping the peninsula safe, Evander was lauded and praised by his summiteer superiors and peers. However, no one was accepting the story that General Dedrick, the Maytoni general in charge, and a royalist, died by Xellcarrian weapons – Maytoni Military Command knew the summiteers too well.

The royalist warmonger had wanted to pursue and obliterate the Xellcarrian forces, and Evander was dead set against further escalation. It could not be proved of course; however, to play it safe, Evander was now in temporary exile until the peace accord with the Xellcarrians was completed. Officially, he had been sent to cross-train with Chanjion archers. Whilst there was no chance that prince Sharrow was going to be handed over to the Xellcarrians, Evander, and his Summiteer kin and kith, had decided they would take care of him, somewhere down the line.

The cross-training with Chanjion archers would help heal his soul, he thought. They were magnificent archers, made more so by the fact that they refused to use magic enhancements of any kind. Yet, duty got in the way and instead of making it to Chanjion, Evander had been sequestered and rerouted to Wetsven, where he now resided with a refreshing lemon water.

An agent, and a good friend, Aeker Murdock had brought intelligence to him. And from Aeker this was a solid as if Evander had made the discovery himself. A fugitive of the Maytoni, known as The Headsman, had been seen off the east coast of the northern sub-continent of The Sigel, and then his presence confirmed when he had been seen in the Wetsven capital.

The Headsman was hardly conspicuous, and in fact not capable of being conspicuous. He was a descendant of giants living in The Scar and stood at eight feet in height. A kill or capture order was in place, with every northern nation – bar Reywher, and of course Wetsven – agreeing to let the Maytoni apprehend the man in their territories. The Headsman was taking a major risk coming back.

Prior to arriving in the capital, the colossus had been hunting in the east of Wetsven. Evander couldn't figure out why. He was far too high profile for any kind of recreation. It had to be connected to his visit to the capital. But there was no way he was looking to join the Flint Castle. For one thing, the poor animal was known as Aldenberg's panther: a sub-species of jaguar with beautiful, sharp, contrasting streaks like lightening scars. No harm to the species, but it was hardly a major trophy. The Fastness had to be his destination.

So, Evander, sat at the marble table with Aeker – who was fussing about the heat and sunlight – watching as the giant took the steps of the Fastness four at a time, his entourage following hastily; three figures in rich leather tunics and breeches, none of whom seemed to be armed. The Headsman carried by his side a large tube of sorts. Clearly looking to hide something, or take something out, Evander mused.

The Shroud Fastness was huge, and its exterior was nothing compared to the city of wealth and secrets beneath it. A rectangular marble structure sat within a perimeter of tall exotic trees, the tops of which seemed to explode in greenery, and a moat of sapphire waters filled with fluttering fish and tall wader birds. On the right of the structure was built a pyramid with a flat top. On the left a hexagonal tower reached upward, taller than the pyramid by half. The top of the tower met with an aqueduct, with water pouring down to the pyramid, and down the whole front of the fastness via a series of golden gutters. During the day it was hardly noticeable, however at night, lamps behind the guttering gave the water a golden glow, presenting a light show of pure gold running along and down the fastness.

"He's using the main entrance..." Aeker muttered, as if The Headsman, a hundred yards away might hear.

"It's the only entrance," Evander added, keeping his eyes on his lemon water, but keeping his focus on The Headsman. "Come on." Evander stood, casually and moved across the cobbled road. Aeker jumped up and jogged to his side. "If things go south, Aeker, bail and get a message back to the Blair Tower," he ordered, sternly. Aeker looked a tad vexed.

"Well, yeah, but I'll come back," he began. Pragmatic to a fault, that was Aeker. He knew the best course of action would be to ensure the summiteers were told of everything that was happening, but he was far from a coward – contrary to his tense, nervy disposition. For an explorer, Aeker was the worst traveller Evander knew. But the fella did it anyway. A testament to the man.

Aeker was six feet tall on the dot, with black hair kept swept back and unkept. Cold blue eyes were set to sparkling by his jet eyebrows and stood out against is ruddy complexion.

"Chasm, Aeker," Evander began as they took to the steps. "I shouldn't even be venturing after this guy without back up. Just get the message out, and then get to safety. No messing about." Evander patted Aeker on the shoulder, winking.

"How often have you fantasied about breaking in here, yeah? Discovering world-shattering secrets, pulling out more wealth than a god would have..."

Aeker was right. This was a major fantasy for every summiteer. So much so that they had often run training simulations, and various scenarios on mock set-ups of the interior – or what their intelligence told them the interior could look like.

"Us, every aspiring thief in the world, and every bored bloke with a few drinks in 'em. Though, even the best thieves are smart enough to not to potentially vex so many powerful figures. Surely this is a fantasy of yours too. All those myths and legends..."

"The trick is getting away with it. I'd say it's not impossible to steal from the Fastness." Aeker was all hand gestures as he spoke. "But come on, when it comes to wealth, or what someone defines as wealth, there's no getting away with it. You'd have better odds assassinating the Emperor of Dytrentia and getting away with it, until your death bed confession."

"Well, brace yourself, Aeker. Because you're not far off taking part in an international incident."

"Not my first, Evey." Aeker grinned back, pushing open the wide red-oak door for him.

The foyer was stunning. Regal portraits, landscapes, and statures sculpted of gold, platinum, and diamond washed the wide, tall room in opulence. Evander was sickened by it. "Nothing corrupts the soul like greed, eh?"

"Those magpie statues are a bit ironic," Aeker said, looking all around him. He wasn't wrong. A bronze carving of a tree stood to their right, reaching fifteen feet in height, with magpies sculpted from onyx, ivory, diamond, sapphire, and emeralds.

"They like shiny things, and so do the twats here." Evander seldom said it aloud, but he found crows to be almost sacred, little messengers from the Gods to keep his spirit going when the darkness in the depths of his psyche tried to consume him.

Officials in gold and purple uniforms wandered about, chatting with clients, or working on parchments behind standing desks. There was no visible security, however Evander knew from experience that it was what you couldn't see that was always far more lethal. He had theories about the magical defences, all summiteers had, and had drilled against them – with scars to prove it. But an inkling told him that a good portion of the Fastness' defences were still unknown to them.

The Headsman was nowhere to be seen.

"Come on. Walk like you're here to see your, vault or whatever, and therefore there is no reason for anyone to stop you, or ask questions," Evander muttered. They rounded the corner of the only other exit and moved further down a vast archway decorated with gilt skirting, a carpet so soft Evander thought he was walking through sand, and more wonderful landscapes. A single man stood, smiling with painful radiance. Through a smooth complexion and bare face, he just looked at Evander and Aeker, saying nothing and waiting for them to speak first.

Behind the guard was a wall of metallic ropes, like metal vines, so intricately woven around and through each other that it looked impossible to trace any one point back to its source.

"Good day, sir," Aeker began. "My friend and I are here to see to our holdings. Is there an issue?" Aeker was an expert suave manipulation, for all his aloofness.

"Certainly, sir. Can I see your confirmation writ, or writ of guardianship?" The guard began cheerfully.

"Yes, here," Evander replied, pulling a scroll from his leather satchel. He was about to hand the forged document over when a hard voice broke over the trio.

"I'll handle this. I'm on my way down, anyway."

Keeping calm and putting on his best look of curiosity, Evander turned to see a woman, five-five, with tied up blonde hair, wearing a violet and deep orange uniform. A pistol was held on the front of her belt, gaudy and bejewelled, and worth more than Evander made in a year.

"Of course, ma'am," the guard replied, pulling his hand away.

Without even offering the writ, this new senior figure took the scroll from Evander and unfurled it. Evander gave a quick look to Aeker who was holding up with concern veiled by a look of curiosity. It had been Evander's brothel owning, underworld savvy, brother who had gotten them the forged writ. They were confident it would work, but there was always the certainty of sod's law to remember.

"Fine day, isn't it?" Aeker chirped. "I'm from the Poet's Sea, we never get the heat... I mean what is it they say about The Sigel? Well placed on the equator, so it's too hot in the north, and too hot in the south. Yeah, trying living in the middle of the Poet's Sea."

Evander give a quick, dull stare. As nervous as Aeker was about the situation, he just had a bad habit of feeling like he had to fill any silences.

"Yes, yes. I'm Matilda Greene, by the way." She didn't take her eyes off the writ. Rather she produced a small ivory and jet pebble from her coat. Evander knew it was a magical device, one used to identify forgeries, and his chest tightened. He didn't think they used this level of security this early on. Then of course, they didn't. It was sod's law intervening in the form of this arbitrary encounter. He hoped his brother had considered such anti-forgery measures but wasn't confident. Violence this soon wasn't good. He had to know why The Headsman was here first.

"Okay..." Matilda looked to Aeker, and grinned. "Grand so." She gave Evander the writ back.

The metallic vines began to untangle rapidly, slithering eerily, each rope disappearing into the frame of the portal. A long corridor, ordained with more landscapes and portraits, was revelled. The floor shimmered as if reflecting golden waters, marble this time.

"A matchlock, I see... I never got them," Aeker began speaking, much to Evander's chagrin. Unfortunately, the guard was moving at a swift pace, and Evander knew it would look suspicious if he and Aeker shot by. "I mean, you get one shot... You can reload, but that takes an age. It's just a loud, unpredictable crossbow, isn't it?"

"It's for show, really," Matilda said, glancing back. "Scares those who don't know weapons... Which you clearly do..." She let that trail off, waiting for Aeker to bluster into a mistake.

"Oh, not really. I just read a lot of history tomes. And well, a lot of history is warfare, isn't it? An understanding of the equipment is important, you know, because it can be a significant part in a victory or a defeat."

"Well, we're not repelling hordes of swamp bandits. Besides, the Fastness is filled with so much sophisticated magic, it's perfectly capable of defending itself."

Nothing Evander didn't know. Even the layout thus far matched summiteer intelligence. He was hoping the Fastness' defences would work to his advantage in apprehending The Headsman. He looked to Matilda, mid-thirties, hard lines to her face, and the kind of eyes that were perpetually scrutinising and analysing. She had probably started in the Wetsven Watch, worked hard enough, or nailed a high-profile enough case for promotion, placing her in this, the most desirable of security posts in the country. In which case, Matilda could be a decent ally. But then, she was still Wetsvenian, and was more likely to declare his own actions illegal and try to apprehend him instead.

They passed a wide fountain, swirling hydra necks rising out of the base, with golden water shooting high into the air. The scales were made of silver and platinum, streaming emerald light gleaming between them. Around the base were carvings of figures carrying trunks and barrels and sacks, in what looked to be a fun little scene of disorganisation.

To the right was a portal, pitch black, and stealing the light around it. A security door of sorts, to prevent anyone looking in where they shouldn't. "This way," Matilda added, quietly.

"A guide, that's new for us," Evander said, also quietly. She was going to make things far too complicated. He made to move through the portal first, however, slightly breaking character.

And there he was. The Headsman, a giant among the human, and elven personal working in this section of Fastness. Bronze hair rolled back from his forehead like a feathered wave, and hard amber eyes glowed like stars behind a foggy night. He was handsome, with high cheek bones and a sharp face.

Several vast, dull steel-coloured slabs stood before The Headsman and his entourage. Behind each door were chambers filled with smaller vaults, however, though most magic was beyond Evander, he knew there was nothing typical about the structure of the Fastness' interior. Stepping through anyone of the steel doors would take Evander to a whole other level underneath the Fastness. Peculiar geometric spells, it made his head hurt to try and think how it all worked.

Evander stopped, but only because Matilda had come to a halt at the top of the bronze steps leading into the room. She half-rose an arm to stop Aeker from walking on.

Another writ was required at this point, one known to be impossible to forge, and of course, an identity check. If The Headsman had a vault here, he was grand. If not, it was about to get bloody and complicated – and Evander did not relish having to sit through officer after officer asking the same questions and him having to repeat the same answers about what happened.

"You look like you're about to reach for that piece," Evander muttered, leaning towards Matilda. Did she know who this was? Was she here to keep an eye on him? Unlikely, on both accounts.

They couldn't hear the conversation, but it was not going anybody's way. The guards were refusing to let The Headsman or his followers any further.

Weaving together through darkening arcs, The Headsman executioner sword was summoned, fitting into the clasps on his back armour. All seven feet of it, fixed down the giant's back, was suddenly glaring at Evander.

"Aeker, get out," he snapped without looking around.

"Ah, well..." Aeker stammered.

"Go!" Evander hissed, and thankfully, that pragmatic common sense came around. Aeker backed out of the room. Matilda glared at Evander, reaching for her pistol. "You're going to have to take my word for it, if not, I'd advise you run too, but I'm here for the big fella." He summoned his bow, which materialized into his left hand, a short recurve, yew, and bamboo with a deep blue kangaroo leather grip. His kangaroo-leather quiver appeared on his waist, filled with maroon, dragon's blood-dyed arrows, replete with navy and indigo arch griffin flights.

"Well, my hunch was right. The magical defences have been disarmed or blocked," Matilda said, looking over Evander's armaments. At the first summons of his bow, Evander knew he should have been struck down by something sudden and painful.

"Blocked most likely, I can't imagine a mage alive who could have the power to disarm all your defensives."

"That bow says Maytoni, and you have no-"

The clasps on The Headsman back armour sprang open, responding to his grip on the lengthy hilt of the tall sword. It was brought down in a single hand, and the poor guard didn't stand a chance. Cleaved in half, both sides crumbled.

Evander loosed an arrow, and the giant spun thrusting out with his sword. Like a moth to a flame, the arrow curved into the flat head of the sword and shattered, despite the dragon's blood strengthening. Abyssal magic ran over the length of the weapon, glistening in darkening shades of black, stealing all ill-will sent towards its wielder, including arrows.

One of the cloaked followers turned enough so Evander could see a vicious snarling maw of metal infused into his lower face, and eyes shot through with painfully red and purple sores. Black, blue, purple, and green veins bulged around the sockets in a grotesque tangle, all the result of decades of reading in major magical knowledge. This fighter's figure fell into shadow, and without moving from the spot, he thrust, cut, and stabbed with a summoned sword. Wounds opened on the guards' throats and chests, and they collapsed in a clatter, eyes wide. One guard, quick enough to have drawn a sword, fell at The Headsman's feet.

Matilda was in shock, her pistol drawn and aimed, however, her hand was trembling. Her mind was caving in, Evander knew, between the horror of what she had seen, and the futility of asserting her authority. It was unlikely that she had delt with anything so bloody, having made a career chasing tax-evaders.

"Maytoni!" The Headsman growled, a tone thick with venom and disgust. Clearly Evander was the last thing he was expecting to see here. "Peasants playing nobles with your silly children's toys!" He kicked a sword at his feet up the steps. It clattered noisily at Evander's feet. "Why not pick up that, a _weapon_, and fight me proper!?"

In defiance, Evander nocked another arrow. The giant's hatred of the Maytoni was well known. "What are you doing here?" Evander ventured, formulating his next move, buying time.

A dozen heavily armoured guards, in purple and gold came rushing and clattering into the room as secret side panels opened on the walls. Tall amber shields filled out in a row between The Headsman and the centre vault, forming a wall which next to the giant seemed to resemble a puny, frail fence. Golden bladed arming swords pointed towards the foes. Now these, Evander knew, had to be proper soldiers, and were exactly who he was waiting for.

Two of the mages turned to engage the soldiers. One manifested multiple arms, ten in all, with spears, swords, and shields. They crashed into the shield wall and instantly began slaughtering the larger part of the guard force. The last mage slithered between the melee and split the tall, wide, steel door in two with a thrust of their hands, before parting the obstacle.

A crack erupted next to Evander as Matilda finally took a shot at The Headsman. The giant kicked up a fallen shield which took the impact. He turned and marched towards the opening, executioner sword over one shoulder, tubed parcel in his other hand. The melee seemed to part for and wash around The Headsman. Evander took aim with another arrow. Then the air in front of him darkened, blurring before turning into a solid pitch, and figure snatched the arrow from his bow. Evander threw his boot out, gut kicking the shade before whipping his dagger out of its waist sheath and plunging it into the mage's neck. He caught the arrow as it tumbled from the mage's grasp, nocked it, and drew on The Headsman as he crossed the portal. Evander loosed, and the arrow was stolen from the air by the leading mage and tossed away as he too jogged after the giant.

Evander began systematically moving and loosing arrows. The multi-armed mage pulled a sword and two spears from three lifeless guards whilst bringing a shield around for cover. Each arrow thumped into it. However, as each arrow struck, the impact of the next was multiplied by the previous one. The mage eventually staggered and began to withdraw through the portal. Matilda, to her credit, moved after him, fumbling with the various components to reload her pistol. She didn't even seem to notice splashing through the rivers of blood leaking out of her dead colleges.

The chamber they swept into was vast, its full size consumed by shadows. Ghostly whisps of luminescence hovered high in the air providing daylight-level illumination. Pyramids of containers filled the chamber with wide lanes between them. Each pyramid was arrayed with stairs and walkways for clients to access their vaults. Rare plants and water features ran ornately around the perimeter of the walkways, giving the structures a palace like attire.

"More sodding opulence," Evander sighed. The excitement of having infiltrated the Shroud Fastness was lost now to the turbulence of the heist. Though Evander had always assumed if he was involved in a heist, he would have been the one robbing the Fastness.

The mage, darkening eyes of violet and harsh red glared at Evander. His torso was swollen with lumpen knots of muscle and tendons from the numerous manifested appendages. It was nauseating to look at, the arms bent and protruding at unnatural angles, writhing as if they held life of their own. Even the level of magic needed for this perverse act sickened Evander, and it baffled him as to why someone would sacrifice their sanity for such grotesque power.

To the left The Headsman and the final mage cut a bloody path through more guards. Gold flashed against abyssal black, and piled up amongst rivers of red.

The mage stalked around Evander and Matilda, keeping his gait as a barrier. Spears, longswords, maces, and shields formed a fortress of defence. Evander's arrows still protruded from one of the round shields.

Matilda raised her pistol. "Please tell me you have something other than that," Evander sighed, glancing at the bejewelled gaudiness which glinted and glistened.

"Because that stick has done so well," she sneered.

"It got us this far," Evander added, holding back a comment about the futility of the Fastness' guards.

The mage launched a spear. Evander tackled Matilda clear of the weapon, her pistol cracking. The shot went wide, and Matilda tumbled over herself. Evander, on one knee began loosing arrows. The mage brought both shields around, however Evander was ready, and had switched to his banshee-arrows. The flights, crypt eagle feathers, had been tied up with strands of flaming red banshee hair. Even the wooden shafts were tainted and faded with slithers of decay present from the undead material. Once loosed, the arrows would cause vibrations in the air at such a pitch that it was beyond most species ability to hear. They would shatter anything of solidity in their wake. Evander sent banshee arrow after banshee arrow thumping into the shields, the vibrations tearing through the structure of the metals, prying them apart. Each shield quickly dissolved into fine dust, and the mage recoiled, his arms flailing in aguish as the reverberations shattered bone and tore flesh into a flurry of pulp.

"Those are a nightmare to make," Evander growled, having used all he had. He rose, nocked a regular arrow – regular by summiteer standards. The mage cast away several of his weapons and summed a pair of bows, held between four hands on either side. It was unsightly, his shooting form like something Evander expected to see from a thespian on stage. Evander bolted to the left, the air whipping past his neck and arms as a detachment's worth of arrows came after him. Whilst four arms held and drew the bows, the others loaded the arrows to ensure there was no break in the rate of shooting.

Evander skirted around the edge of a vault, arrows clanging off the corner. He clambered up the side of the container, flattening himself onto the roof. Matilda was still down there somewhere, and he hoped she had the sense to get out of there. Yet another crack told him otherwise. He rose and loosed, the arrow striking the mage in the chest as he turned to face the pistoleer. The knots of muscles and bone protruding from the mage's torso, to work the arms, functioned like a type of armour. Matilda took the opportunity, drawing a lengthy dagger from under her coat. She leapt amongst the flail of arms. Evander lost sight of her, but the spray of ruby fluid told him Matilda had gotten in a killing stroke.

The mage collapsed in a grotesque heap. Matilda stood next to him, hands on knees and panting heavily. She cast a very unamused glare at Evander, who gave her a thumbs up and grin. _Good on you,_ he thought. He clambered off the vault and tore after The Headsman, over the fallen guards and through the slush of gore.

Following the dead, Evander came to a wall of vaults, a single row, before which stood The Headsman; the executioners sword leaning over one balustrade of a shoulder. The final mage had unfurled a length of animal hide from the tube. Rich brown fractal patters reached out across the golden hide, like branches or capillaries. The Aldenberg's panther, an obscure jaguar species, named for the infamous, and late, game hunter.

A snort, somewhere between the rumble of a gorilla and bull, came from The Headsman and he turned on the spot. Surprisingly soft eyes met Evander's, the hatred of all things Maytoni darkening the amber irises. The Headsman turned his sword, blade down, the flat top digging into the floor, and stood holding the immense weapon like a staff.

Matilda ran up beside Evander and didn't hesitate to take aim and pulled the trigger. A clack was followed by complete silence. Misfire.

A dark smirk, like a deep scar cut across The Headsman's face. "Like it would have mattered. That little ball would have been eaten by my sword."

"You can't possibly take on the whole of the Fastness," Evander spoke, watching as the mage fixed the animal hide into the door of a vault. "You can get into that vault, but what's your exit strategy?" Evander knew that on the surface the odds were against The Headsman. But, in the back of his mind, he knew it couldn't be that simple.

The mage began to trace along specific lines of the fractal pattern, and it dawned on Evander why The Headsman had been hunting the cat species. "A striking pattern, Maytoni, but more than a random series of stripes," The Headsman spoke, growling, his temper barely constrained. "The key to this lock was found on this species of cat."

Through a breath, like a dragon wheezing, the vault door unsealed itself and rolled open. The same type of abyssal wall which Evander had passed through earlier shielded the interior from view.

"Secure them," The Headsman ordered the mage, keeping his searing stare on Evander.

"What are you after? There's got to be easier ways to get access to someone's vault," Evander kept his thumb around the string of his bow, and kept his breathing steady, forcing his heart rate to drop. That sword would come around like a lightning strike and take the arrow, and he wasn't confident about his odds in close combat. They needed more guards, but where were they? Sprawled out and lifeless behind them, Evander thought.

"Something which will purge you Maytoni from the face of the world – every person, every building, every patch of land tainted by your vile kind!" He barked, spittle flying from his mouth, the hate filled words thick in acid, dripping with contempt.

"Well, I'll just wait. Because your mage will have to come out this way, and we'll see," Evander said, nonchalantly. He was trying to play it cool, though his mind was racing over every possible eventuality for how The Headsman was planning to get out of this. He wasn't bluffing, he was far too confident, and sure of himself. The Headsman had a plan, and Evander was beginning to weave together a possibility, as extravagant as it was...

And there was now this new threat. The Headsman hated Maytoni, not just the Church, the beliefs, but everything: its history, their Gods, the country, Evander's, and his people's very existence. The Headsman had hunted down and tortured pastorals, incited acts of terrorism within the country in the past, but never had the resources to carryout anything major, such as the harm which could come from a full-scale war, or genocide. Anytime summiteers had been dispatched to apprehend, or assassinate him, The

Headsman either escaped them, or cut them down.

Now this bold threat. The vaults of the Shroud Fastness held Gods only knew what among the riches and heirlooms, and frankly legitimate stuff. There were rumours, myths, horror stories; the final remains of cultures, civilisations, and religions kept hostage by Dytrentia, or the remains of legitimate heirs to various thrones kept hidden.

"If we meet again, Maytoni, you'll be a corpse. One of millions. Not one of you will remain." The Headsman turned and marched into the abyssal wall. Evander knew it. Portal magic: unstable, unpredictable, but it could be temporarily controlled. Only a handful of mages the world over could manage it.

Whatever harm The Headsman had inflicted on Maytoni in the past, he was more than serious about enacting this threat. This wasn't a chest pounding, extravagant show of force, he had a plan to see the whole of Maytoni obliterated.

Evander charged after The Headsman, readying his dagger. He leapt through the abyssal wall, and came down swinging into open air, into an empty vault. A numb shock took Evander, a disbelief that he was too late. Surely, somewhere within the bare room, was The Headsman. Ice tingled at his cheeks and burned down his neck. He composed himself quickly, however.

Nothing remained. Not even a trace of the portal magic.

Rising fires within his chest, Evander marched back out of the vault. Matilda was flustered, panting heavily as the adrenaline wore off. He'd have to act fast before she became useless to him. Snapping his fingers to get her attention, he spoke, firm but not aggressively, "Hey, hey. Who owns this vault? Matilda!"

She met his hard forest green eyes, then marched over to the vault. From inside her coat she pulled a scroll, unfurled it, and held to up to a string character on the doorframe. The owner's details formed in ink over the parchment.

Orion's desk was so smooth, a gorgeous slab of rock-bark. Even the chair was very comfy. Luciana had yet to think of any of it as hers, despite the fact that everything Orion had owned went to her in his will. Orion's trophies still mounted the walls, the quad tusk mammoth skull, the massive back fin from a giant lizard, the skulls, hides, and furs over the walls and held in cases. Even the hydra was still blocking out the full light from the tall, wide window overlooking the private hunting ground of Castle.

Her quiet reverie, or smouldering rather, was interrupted by the muffled commotion from the other side of the office's tall door; shouting, as if coming through water took Luci's attention, her eyes glancing up and holding on the door.

The shouting stopped then, abruptly. A hard thud then reverberated through door. Then another, and another. Then silence for a second, before the door opened and a man, marched in, panting, flushed, and dishevelled to say the least. Hard forest green eyes sat under unkept blonde hair. The stranger held a gorgeous yew and bamboo bow, with a quiver of arch-griffin feathered arrows, swaying from his waist.

"Luciana Doran," he gasped, hurriedly. "We need to talk."

Printed by Amazon Italia Logistica S.r.l.
Torrazza Piemonte (TO), Italy

68907814R00131